DEATH AT THE DOG PARK

TWO NOVELLAS

NEIL PLAKCY
JOANNA CAMPBELL SLAN

spot on publishing

Death at the Dog Park: Dog's Punishment. Copyright 2025 Neil S. Plakcy. This book is a work of fiction. Names, characters, places, and incidents either are products of the author's imagination or are used fictitiously. Any resemblance to actual events or locales or persons, living or dead, is entirely coincidental.

All rights reserved, including the right of reproduction in whole or in part in any form.

Death at the Dog Park: Lamb Chopped. Copyright 2025 by Joanna Campbell Slan. This book is a work of fiction. Names, characters, places, and incidents either are products of the author's imagination or are used fictitiously. Any resemblance to actual events or locales or persons, living or dead, is entirely coincidental.

All rights reserved, including the right of reproduction in whole or in part in any form

A NOTE FROM NEIL AND JOANNA

Writing is a lonely business, and the longer you're in it, the harder it gets. We decided to talk to each other weekly to share ideas, cheer each other on, and hold each other accountable. It made sense because we both write series fiction about dogs and dog owners in that genre known as cozies, a term for traditional mysteries. Then we had a crazy idea: Why not use our individual series, start with the same prompt—"death in a dog park"—and create two novellas (short books) that would appeal to both our audiences? And this is the result. We hope you have as much enjoyment reading this as we did writing it.

Neil Plakcy, Hollywood, Florida
Joanna Campbell Slan, Jupiter Island, Florida.

CONTENTS

DOG'S PUNISHMENT

1. Bad Influence	3
2. A Hard Hit	8
3. Photo Session	14
4. Nittany Lions	21
5. Neighborhood Watch	29
6. The Chocolate Ear	32
7. The Husband	37
8. Pawsitive Solutions	41
9. Best in Show	46
10. Obedience Trials	51
11. Follow the Money	55
12. Charmed	61
13. Business Development	66
14. Palatial Drive	70
15. Digital Eyes	77
16. Those Who Can't Speak	82
Neil's Author Notes & Free Gift	89

LAMB CHOPPED

Chapter 1	93
Chapter 2	94
Chapter 3	96
Chapter 4	99
Chapter 5	104
Chapter 6	109
Chapter 7	114
Chapter 8	117
Chapter 9	120
Chapter 10	123
Chapter 11	128

Chapter 12	133
Chapter 13	136
Chapter 14	141
Chapter 15	144
Chapter 16	150
Chapter 17	152
Chapter 18	158
Chapter 19	161
Chapter 20	166
Chapter 21	168
Chapter 22	173
Chapter 23	175
Chapter 24	180
Joanna's Author Note & Free Gift!	183
About Joanna Campbell Slan—	185

DOG'S PUNISHMENT

A GOLDEN RETRIEVER MYSTERY

by Neil S. Plakcy

1. BAD INFLUENCE

My golden retriever Rochester and I were out for our dinnertime walk on a summer evening in 2015, shortly after his fourth birthday, when we rounded a corner and he spotted his second-best friend, an English Cream golden named Brody. Immediately I had 90 pounds of fur and muscle dragging me forward, no matter what I said to stop him.

"Your dog is a very bad influence on mine," I said, as I finally gave up and let go of Rochester's lead, and he bounded forward toward my friend and co-worker Joey Capodilupo.

Joey let go of Brody's leash at the same time, and the two dogs rushed into each other in a mad jumble of gold and white fur. Rochester was bigger and older, but Brody was a spoiled little bully, trying to hump my dog. Rochester squirmed out from underneath him and went down on his front paws in the play position.

"We're taking him for obedience lessons," Joey said. "Again. But Melissa Kawamoto comes highly recommended for her work with older dogs."

Joey and I shared management duties at Eastern College's

Friar Lake Conference Center. I handled programming and finance, while he took care of all the buildings and grounds. It was a great division of duties—Joey was a strapping guy in his thirties, a former college baseball player who handled almost any repairs on the property. Though I was six-one, he had at least four inches on me, which meant he changed light bulbs and dusted the stained-glass windows in the chapel without a ladder.

"Brody's not exactly elderly," I said. "He's what, two years old by now?"

"Yup. But Melissa says a lot of bad habits get locked in during puppyhood."

It was a warm evening in late August, with a tiny nip in the air that reminded me that fall was coming. That meant it had been just over a year since Joey and his partner Mark had bought a townhouse in River Bend, the community where my wife Lili and I lived with Rochester. Sometimes we commuted together, and we took each other's dogs in when the humans went on vacation.

One of the nice things about River Bend is the empty lots between pods of townhouses, and that's where Rochester and Brody were romping. Watching a golden retriever run is poetry in motion. Their long legs churn, and their fur stands up in the breeze like Tibetan prayer flags. They raced back and forth, darting around shrubs and occasionally stopping to pee.

"Melissa's running a free clinic tomorrow morning at the dog park downtown," Joey said. "I'd like him to calm down enough that he could spend time with Mark at the antique shop without destroying anything."

Mark Figueroa ran a shop in the center of town with a little of everything—whatever he'd been able to find at yard sales and charity shops that he could make a small profit on. He and Joey both loved to refinish old furniture—Joey did the carpentry work like fashioning new legs for an old chair, while Mark polished and painted.

"You think she can handle him?"

Joey shrugged. "I hope so. We've tried every other trainer in the area. We spent a fortune with a company called Pawsitive Solutions and all that happened was Brody started to gain weight from all the treats we were giving him."

Brody and Rochester continued to play, chasing each other and barking, until the automatic sprinklers came on, and both dogs rushed back toward us.

"You should bring Rochester to the clinic tomorrow morning," Joey said. "It's free, and I'd be curious to see what you and Rochester think of her."

I thought my dog was perfectly behaved, but he did have a tendency to overwhelm me sometimes. "Sounds good." I didn't offer to drive us because I didn't want Brody encouraging Rochester to go wild in my SUV.

"What time is the clinic?"

"It starts at eight," Joey said.

"I'll meet you there, then," I said. Rochester and I turned toward home.

"Did you have a good time with your friend?" I asked once we were on our own.

Rochester panted and smiled, his long tongue hanging out. It could have meant he was happy—but then again, he was hot from all that exercise. Dogs only had sweat glands in their paw pads and their noses, so panting was a primary way for them to cool off after exertion.

When we got home, Rochester drank copiously from his water bowl and then came up close to my leg. "I love you, but I'm not your napkin, dog," I said, gently pushing him away. Lili was reading on the sofa, so I sat at the dining room table with my laptop and checked out Melissa Kawamoto's website.

The front page featured an image of a man and a woman holding hands, walking down a country road. A chocolate lab strode off-leash beside the man. The caption beneath the photo was "Turning Reactive Dogs into Perfect Companions."

The text read, "A reactive dog is one that overreacts to normal situations, such as people, other dogs, or noises. Reactive dogs can be fearful, frustrated, or excited, and their reactions can include barking, lunging, or growling. While reactive dogs aren't necessarily aggressive, reactivity can sometimes lead to aggression. We teach owners to help their dogs cope with these stimuli."

I sat back in my chair. It was an interesting idea, and I wondered what methods Melissa used in her training. Maybe Rochester and I would learn something at her free clinic.

I took him for one last walk before bedtime, and we ran into a woman and her Yorkie who we saw occasionally. The dog began barking and growling as soon as he saw Rochester, but the woman ignored his behavior, concentrating on something on her phone. The tiny dog was so excited that he pulled and jumped to get toward us. I was tempted to tell the woman about the clinic the next morning, but I doubted she'd listen.

The next day was Saturday, and you'd think I'd be able to sleep in, but Rochester's inner clock didn't work that way. Every morning for him was a chance to get out and discover fresh smells and new pee-mail left by neighbor dogs.

After a quick walk, I bundled him into my SUV and drove into the center of Stewart's Crossing. The morning sun lit up the Delaware River, which curved past our town like a silver ribbon. Colonial-era stone buildings and Carpenter Gothic homes lined the narrow streets, their gardens still bright with late-summer flowers.

Dew clung heavily to the grass at the dog park. I checked my watch as I pulled into the nearly empty parking lot. Seven-forty-five—plenty of time before Melissa Kawamoto's free training clinic was scheduled to start at eight.

Rochester's tail thumped against the back seat as I killed the engine. My golden retriever knew something special was in store, though he didn't know what. Perhaps he expected that we'd head for coffee at the Chocolate Ear Café, which always meant special dog biscuits for him.

But today's schedule would be different, assuming Melissa showed up on time with her demonstration of "alpha dog" training techniques.

I hadn't decided yet whether I agreed with the criticism surrounding her methods. According to the local dog training community's gossip—which I'd heard only in passing—Melissa's approach was unnecessarily harsh. But I figured I should see for myself before making any judgments.

My hand was on the door handle when I noticed the police cruiser partially hidden behind the park's maintenance shed. A familiar figure in plain clothes stood next to it, speaking into his phone: Rick Stemper. My best friend, and the Stewart's Crossing police detective most experienced in homicide investigation.

2. A HARD HIT

"Hold on, boy," I said as Rochester whined softly. That's when I saw the yellow crime scene tape fluttering in the breeze, cordoning off the park's main training area.

Rick spotted me and ended his call, walking over as I got out of the car. Rochester hopped out behind me and pressed against my leg, unusually subdued.

"Morning, Steve," Rick said, his expression grim. "Guess you were planning to attend the clinic?"

I nodded. "What happened?"

"An early-morning jogger found Melissa Kawamoto's body about half an hour ago and called 911. The body is over by the agility equipment." Rick gestured toward a cluster of uniformed officers. "ME's on the way, but it looks like she took a hard hit to the head."

Rochester's ears perked up, and he turned toward the crime scene, nose twitching. I felt the familiar tension in the leash that usually meant my dog had caught an interesting scent.

"Any signs of robbery?" I asked, studying the empty park.

Dog's Punishment

The morning sun cast long shadows across the wet grass, and a light mist still hung in the air.

"Nothing obvious missing. Her car's in the lot, phone's not on her. She might have slipped in the dew and hit her head on one of the equipment pieces." Rick didn't sound entirely convinced. "Though I've got to say, your boy's behavior makes me wonder if there's more to it."

Rochester had moved into what I recognized as his alert posture, head low and tail straight. Whatever he was sensing, it wasn't the usual morning park smells.

"Mind if we take a closer look?" I asked, knowing from experience that Rochester's instincts often proved valuable in Rick's investigations.

Rick sighed, but I saw the slight smile playing at the corners of his mouth. "Why do I even bother asking you to stay out of my cases anymore? Come on—but stay behind the tape. And Steve? Watch where Rochester sniffs. Something tells me this isn't going to be the simple accident it looks like."

Rochester led me along the perimeter of the crime scene, his nose working overtime. Near the tunnel obstacle, he stopped abruptly, head lowered. His tail went rigid.

"What is it, boy?"

He pawed at something in the wet grass. Squinting, I spotted a partial footprint in the mud—too deep for someone just walking past. Next to it lay a small silver charm shaped like a dog bone. A piece of broken chain dangled from one end.

"Rick," I called softly. "You might want to see this."

My friend crouched down, straining the knees of his cargo pants. He pulled an evidence bag from the leg pocket. "Well, well. Our victim was wearing a charm bracelet when she was found. This piece looks like it came off that."

Rochester maintained his alert stance, eyes fixed on the footprint. Someone had stood here long enough to leave a deep impression—and possibly long enough to commit murder.

Rick left us to grab a handful of short metal stakes and yellow crime scene tape from his car. "Good catch," he said when he returned. "We'll need photos before anyone else walks through here." He circled the evidence with stakes, creating a smaller perimeter within the larger crime scene. "The rain's supposed to hold off until tonight, but I want this footprint cast as soon as possible."

Rochester stayed focused on the spot while Rick radioed for the crime scene unit. I noticed my dog's nose twitching toward a cluster of bushes about ten feet away, but Rick was already waving us back. "That's enough detecting for now, you two. Let me get this processed properly."

A car door slammed in the parking lot, followed by excited barking. I turned to see Sarah Ramsey wrestling with her chocolate Labrador retriever, Cocoa, who was practically dragging her toward the training area.

She was a trim woman in her mid-thirties who liked to wear dog-related T-shirts over long, flowy white skirts, matched up with Doc Martens boots. "Steve!" she called out, then stopped short when she saw the police tape. "Oh no. What's happened?"

Before I answered, Cocoa lunged forward, nearly pulling Sarah off her feet. The Lab was wearing one of those prong collars I'd seen on badly behaved dogs, but it didn't seem to be helping much.

"Melissa Kawamoto was found dead this morning," I said quietly.

Sarah's hand flew to her mouth. "Dead? But I have an appointment with her next week. She was supposed to help me with Cocoa." Her voice cracked slightly. "I know some people thought her methods were harsh, but I'm desperate. Cocoa's destroyed our couch, two chairs, and Ian's expensive running shoes. He's threatening to make me give her up."

I watched as Cocoa strained at the leash, barking at a squirrel. Rochester sat calmly at my side, and I felt a surge of gratitude for his steady temperament.

"I've tried positive reinforcement trainers," Sarah continued, wiping her eyes. "But nothing works. Melissa said she could fix Cocoa in three sessions." She looked at the crime scene. "What happened to her?"

Rick had stepped away to take another call, so I just shook my head. "They're still investigating."

More cars were pulling into the lot now, and people were getting out with dogs on leashes. I saw the humans checking their phones, probably wondering why the entrance to the training area was blocked.

Sarah struggled with Cocoa, who was still barking at the squirrel. "I should get her home before she drives everyone crazy. But please tell Rick to let me know if there's anything I can do to help. Melissa may have been controversial, but she was trying to help people like me."

As Sarah led her still-pulling Lab away, I heard another familiar bark. Joey's truck had arrived, and Brody was practically climbing out the passenger window, his white fur glowing in the morning sun. Joey parked next to my SUV and got out, his face falling as he saw the crime scene tape. He held Brody on a short leash, which didn't make his little dog very happy.

"Steve? What's going on?" He was wearing running clothes – shorts and a Penn State baseball t-shirt – and there were sweat marks around his neck and under his arms.

Rick walked over before I answered. "Mr. Capodilupo. Back so soon?"

Joey's expression shifted from confusion to wariness. "What do you mean?"

"Your truck was spotted in the lot around six this morning," Rick said. "Security camera at the convenience store across the street."

I looked at my friend and co-worker with surprise. Joey was an early riser – he often talked about hitting the gym before work – but I'd never known him to bring Brody to the park that early.

Brody was barking and straining to get close to Rochester. Instead of joining in the play, my golden slumped to the ground and stared at his friend, as if willing him to shut up and calm down.

"Yeah, I was here," Joey said, running a hand through his short black hair. "I drove by the park around six looking for Melissa. But there was another car here, so I went to get breakfast instead. Brody gets... overexcited around other dogs. That's why we were going to work with Melissa one-on-one." His voice caught slightly on her name. "Why? What happened?"

"Where did you go for breakfast?" Rick asked, ignoring the question.

"The Sunoco on Ferry. I needed to fill up and I like their sandwiches. I have the receipt somewhere." Joey looked from Rick to me, then back to the crime scene where the cluster of officers still stood. "Is that... oh God, is that Melissa?"

Rochester whined softly and pressed against my leg. I'd known Joey for years, worked with him every day. I couldn't believe Rick was treating him like a suspect. But then again, he had been here early, during what the police would call the probable time of death.

"We'll need a formal statement," Rick said. "Remember we've got that security footage so make sure you take that into account."

"Of course," Joey said. "Whatever you need." He swallowed hard. "But I swear, when we left, the only car I saw besides

Melissa's was a blue Prius." He paused for a moment. "Look, can I take Brody home? He's getting agitated, and Mark will need to open the shop soon. I said I would help him this morning."

Rick nodded. "We'll be in touch about that statement."

As Joey led Brody back to his truck, Rochester watched them intently. My dog had known Brody all the puppy's life, played with him regularly. But something about either Joey or his dog had captured Rochester's attention in a way I'd never seen before.

I wondered if Rick had noticed it too. And what exactly had happened in the park.

3. PHOTO SESSION

The rich aroma of Cuban coffee filled our kitchen as I walked in through the front door. Rochester took one sniff and retreated to the living room, because he'd never developed a taste for the strong smell of Lili's morning café Cubano.

She stood at the counter, listening to the steam rising from her espresso machine. Although she had long since retired as a photojournalist in favor of heading the Fine Arts Department at Eastern College, and teaching the occasional course, she kept her hand in by taking photographs. She was already dressed for a morning shoot, her camera bag packed and waiting by the door. Her effusive auburn curls had been pulled back in a practical ponytail, but a few strands had escaped to frame her face.

"You're back early," she said, turning to give me a kiss. Then she saw my expression. "What's wrong?"

I sank into one of our kitchen chairs. "A dog trainer named Melissa Kawamoto was found dead at the dog park this morning."

"Melissa?" Lili's hand flew to her mouth. "Oh no. I just spoke to her last week about updating her website photos."

"You knew her?"

"I took pictures for her flyers when she started her training service." Lili moved the coffee off the heat and poured two small cups. "She wanted action shots of her working with different breeds. I remember thinking how confident she was, even with the more aggressive dogs."

I wrapped my fingers around the tiny cup, letting the strong coffee's warmth seep in. "Did she ever mention having problems with anyone? Threats?"

"Not exactly threats." Lili sat across from me in the morning light streaming through our kitchen window. "But she was worried about something. When she called about new photos, she said she needed to rebrand quickly. Something about her reputation being attacked online."

Through the doorway, I saw Rochester lying in his favorite spot by the sliding glass doors that looked out to the courtyard, but his head was up, listening to our conversation.

"She didn't say who was behind the attacks?"

Lili shook her head. "But she mentioned taking legal action. She wanted the new photos to look more professional, more corporate. Said she was planning to expand her business." She paused. "Steve, what happened to her?"

I told her about finding the body, about Rick's investigation, about Joey being there earlier. With each detail, Lili's expression grew more concerned.

"I have all the photos from our session," she said. "The ones she used and the ones she didn't. Maybe there's something in the backgrounds, something that could help?"

"That's worth checking. I want to look into these online attacks she mentioned."

Lili glanced at her watch. "I have to get to my shoot. It's for an engagement announcement and they want to include their golden retriever, who was getting a professional bath and blow dry this morning. But I'll dig out Melissa's photo files when I get back."

After Lili left, I pulled out my hacker laptop and settled at the dining room table. I had some solid computer search skills, as well as a number of less-than-legitimate programs that helped me search the dark web, and I'd often used my skills and those programs to help Rick with his investigations.

Rochester followed, flopping down in his bed in the corner, but I could tell he wasn't really sleeping. His ears twitched at every sound, and occasionally he'd lift his head and stare at me as if trying to communicate something important.

I pulled up Google and typed "Melissa Kawamoto dog trainer." This time I went beyond the front-page photo and caption, and jumped to the "about" page.

Her profile picture showed a woman in her mid-thirties with straight black hair pulled back in a ponytail, demonstrating a sit-stay with a German Shepherd. The dog's attention was completely focused on her, exactly what you'd want to see from a trainer. She had a degree in Animal Science from Penn State and had spent several years training dogs, both as a hobby and eventually as a professional. She had passed all the exams offered by the Certification Council for Professional Dog Trainers, including the Certified Professional Dog Trainer-Knowledge Assessed. That designation measured a broad range of knowledge and skills in the science of animal behavior, learning theory, dog training technique, and instruction.

I jumped to a review site called petcare.org, where the comments were mixed. Many were glowing:

"Melissa saved our relationship with our dog."

"Finally, someone who understands that not every dog responds to treats and baby talk!"

"Worth every penny – our German Shepherd is like a different dog now."

But scattered among the praise were some disturbing comments:

"*Cruel and unnecessary methods.*"

"*My dog was traumatized.*"

"*Stay away if you actually love your pet.*"

One review caught my eye:

"Ms. Kawamoto's methods are derivative of established pressure-point techniques. Her so-called innovations merely build on existing patents, including my own." It was signed Colin Whitaker, former VP of Engineering, PetTech Industries

Below that, another user had commented: "Don't listen to Whitaker. He's bitter because David Bloom dropped him as an investment client when Melissa developed something better."

Whitaker had replied: "Mr. Bloom would do well to remember who developed the original technology. Some of us have long memories about intellectual property."

The exchange had happened six months ago, right around the time Melissa incorporated Alpha Dog Training LLC. I made a note to look into both Whitaker and his connection to David Bloom. Anyone that bitter about patent rights was worth investigating.

Several posts by a user identified as anonymous_4321 went beyond criticism into something darker:

"*She doesn't deserve to work with animals. Someone should stop her.*"

"*Karma will catch up with her eventually. Dogs remember who hurts them.*"

"*Watch your back, Melissa. What goes around comes around.*"

The last post was dated three days ago.

I started taking notes, cross-referencing names from the positive reviews with local dog training clubs and competition records. In her past work, Melissa had accumulated an impressive list of clients whose dogs had earned obedience titles. But the negative reviews seemed to cluster around the last six months, right around the time she'd parted ways with a company called Pawsitive Solutions.

That name rang a bell, and I recalled Joey had mentioned training Brody with them. Had he worked with Melissa then? But he'd said their training only made Brody fat. It didn't make sense that he'd continue to work with her.

I pushed that thought aside. A quick check of business records showed that Patricia Morgan had founded Pawsitive Solutions five years ago. It was an LLC registered to an address in Stewart's Crossing, and I checked Google Maps to look at it.

Photos of the address showed a Victorian house with an enclosed wraparound porch, on a big piece of land. The front yard was subdivided into several fenced areas. From what I'd seen from other trainers, that kind of separation allowed dogs of different sizes to exercise and be trained safely.

From various social media sites, I deduced that Melissa had worked there for eight months, until an abrupt shift six months before when she announced she was striking out on her own. She updated her socials regularly, soliciting clients with a combination of text instructions and photos of well-behaved dogs.

I went back to the anonymous threats. The posts had been made through a throwaway account, but every modern device left digital fingerprints. If I could trace those posts back to their source, I'd have something worth showing Rick.

The whole point of anonymous mode is that it's *not easy* for an administrator or moderator to figure out who posted it. To link a real user to an anonymous account, you have to do some digging, likely checking IP addresses, writing styles, last seen times, and more.

You'd think by 2015 every internet site would have strong security, but that wasn't the case. Sites that didn't collect sensitive information, like account numbers or social security identifiers, were often lax on their security measures. Fortunately for me, petcare.org was one of those.

I had a tool that cracked into administrator mode on such sites, and I was able to get into petcare.org as an admin. I discovered that it was more of a hobby site than a commercial one, run by a dog breeder in Arkansas.

I wrote a query to the database asking for identification of anonymous_4321, which revealed the IP address behind it. Unfortunately, it was an IP address that I recognized because I occasionally used it myself, when I wanted to hide my identity. It was registered to the Stewart's Crossing Public Library.

When I was a kid, the library was housed in a Carpenter Gothic house on Ferry Street, north of downtown. While I was away in New York and California, taxpayers had raised a bond to remodel it, tearing down a non-descript house next door and building a brick expansion. Big windows let in a lot of light, and books were stacked on metal shelves that separated them into fiction and non-fiction.

Behind the foreign-language section, instituted after an influx of immigrants to the area, a row of tables with computers had been set up. Though porn sites and other questionable addresses were restricted, otherwise you could use the computers for whatever you needed. I often saw elderly people using them for email and teens doing school research.

While it was a kind of dead end, at least I'd narrowed down the identity of anonymous_4321 to someone in the greater Stewart's Crossing area. In other words, somebody local had been threatening Melissa.

My phone buzzed with a text from Rick: "Need to talk. Reviewing surveillance footage from the convenience store. Can you and Rochester meet me at the station?"

I looked at my notes, then at Rochester, who was still

watching the door. "Come on, boy," I said. "Let's go see what else you can tell us about this morning."

4. NITTANY LIONS

Rochester's tail started wagging as soon as we walked into the Stewart's Crossing Police Station. The desk sergeant looked up from his paperwork and smiled. "There's my favorite detective," he said, reaching into his desk drawer for the box of organic dog biscuits he kept there.

Rochester sat politely, though his tail thumped against the linoleum floor. After making him wait for the requisite few seconds, the sergeant held out a biscuit. "Such a gentleman," he said. "Unlike some of the officers around here."

"Is Rick ready for us?" I asked.

He nodded toward the detective squad room. "He's reviewing security footage. Fair warning. He's not in the best mood."

Rochester finished his treat and led the way to Rick's desk. My friend was hunched over his computer screen, his tie loosened and his normally neat dark hair showing signs of frequent finger-combing.

"Thanks for coming in," he said, not looking up. "I've been watching Joey's truck on the convenience store's security camera." Rick clicked his mouse, and a grainy image appeared on the screen. "Time stamp shows 6:22 AM." He pointed to three vehicles in the dog park lot: Joey's pickup truck, a blue Prius, and a dark-colored SUV with an "Alpha Dog Training" magnetic sign on the door. "That's Melissa's vehicle. The next footage is ten minutes later, and the only car remaining is Melissa's."

Rochester had moved closer to the screen, his nose twitching. I wondered if he smelled something different about Rick's mood. My friend seemed more tense than usual.

"Joey said there was another car besides Melissa's in the lot," I said. "He didn't want Brody to mix it up with another dog, so he left."

"So he says." Rick leaned back in his chair. "Here's the thing—we found partial prints on the charm bracelet piece. They're not clear enough for a definitive match, but the size and pattern are consistent with work gloves. The kind Joey wears at Friar Lake."

My stomach tightened. "Come on, Rick. Joey's not a killer."

"The medical examiner puts time of death between 6:15 and 6:45. Joey admits being there. He knew about Melissa's training methods, had access to the park early in the morning, and was strong enough to deliver the fatal blow."

"But why would he kill her? He hoped to be her client."

Rick pulled up another window on his computer. "Her brother provided us with access to her business receipts," he said. "According to them, Joey had already paid for six private sessions with Melissa. But last week, she refunded his money. The transaction memo says, 'Services terminated by trainer.'"

Rochester whined softly and pressed against my leg. I reached down to scratch his ears, trying to process what Rick was telling me.

Joey was patient with Brody, even when the dog was impossibly energetic. He was eager to improve his dog's behavior. Why would Melissa have canceled those training sessions? Why was

Joey going to the free session then? And why would he have recommended her to me?

Rick rubbed his eyes. "Look, I know Joey's your friend. But right now, he's not being straight with us."

Rochester had moved to the window, watching traffic on the street below. His posture was alert but not tense.

"I found a number of threatening posts online," I said. "I did some snooping, and the negative ones were posted anonymously from the Stewart's Crossing library IP address."

"Which is down the street from Mark Figueroa's antique shop," Rick said. "Where Joey spends a lot of time. His presence at the scene, the glove prints... it's adding up to something I don't like."

I thought about the Joey I knew, the guy who did everything that was asked of him, and more. Who'd spent a whole weekend helping Lili and me paint our living room. Who was kind and patient with his rambunctious dog. "There has to be another explanation."

"I hope you're right." Rick stood up and stretched. "Because I have called your friend in for questioning. And Steve? I need you to stay out of it. This is official police business."

Rochester turned from the window and gave a soft woof. Through the glass wall of the detective squad room, I saw the desk sergeant talking to someone at the front desk. Someone with a white-furred dog straining at the leash.

Joey had come in to make his statement. From the look on his face when he spotted me through the glass, he knew exactly how much trouble he was in.

I had to pass through the front desk area to leave, and that meant coming face to face with Joey and Brody. The white golden pulled at his leash as soon as he saw Rochester, tail wagging, ready to play as always. But Rochester, who normally would have been excited to see his friend, stayed pressed against my leg. He didn't even acknowledge Brody's playful bark.

What on earth was Rochester trying to tell me?

Joey wouldn't meet my eyes. He stood there in his running clothes, still sweaty from his morning workout, holding Brody's leash with white-knuckled hands. Rochester and I had to squeeze past my friend and his dog to reach the door. I heard Joey take a shaky breath as if about to speak. But what could either of us say?

I left the station. There was nothing more I could do there, and I needed time to think. Rochester seemed to sense my mood, because he was unusually quiet on the drive home, only occasionally glancing at me in the rearview mirror with those soulful brown eyes that seemed to understand everything.

Back home, my thoughts kept returning to Joey's presence at the park that morning. Something wasn't adding up, but I couldn't put my finger on the missing piece. Rochester seemed restless too, moving from one sliding glass door to the other instead of settling down for his usual afternoon nap.

I was about to turn on my computer when Rochester trotted into the laundry room. A moment later, I heard something being scooted around. He'd made this noise before when he was rummaging around in the dirty clothes.

"What have you got there, boy?" I called to him.

Rochester emerged with a navy-blue t-shirt in his mouth, tail wagging slowly. This was his "I found something important" wag. It was Joey's shirt, left here the weekend before when he'd helped me install a new water heater. The shirt was damp from Rochester's mouth, but I spotted the Penn State logo and "Class of 2005" beneath it.

That triggered something in my memory. I turned back to my computer and pulled up Melissa's LinkedIn profile. There it was: Bachelor's in Animal Science from Penn State, Class of 2005. The same year as Joey.

Spurred by this new bit of information, I dug deeper. Penn State's alumni database was public, and it didn't take long to find yearbook photos. Joey and Melissa were both members of the Pre-Vet Club. In one photo, they stood next to each other at a club fundraiser, smiling broadly with a German Shepherd puppy sitting between them.

Why had Melissa refunded his training fees if they were old friends? Why hadn't Joey mentioned knowing her from college? Why keep going to her training sessions after she'd dismissed him as a client? Had he gone to the training at the park to convince her to take him and Brody on as clients one more time?

Rochester dropped the shirt at my feet and whined. He had that look he gets when he's trying to tell me something important.

"What is it, boy? What else do you know about Joey and Melissa?"

The dog picked up the shirt again and headed for the front door. Whatever he wanted to show me, it wasn't in the house. I took the shirt from his mouth, grabbed my keys, and put on his leash.

He turned left, moving rapidly, not stopping to sniff and pee as he usually did. I let him take the lead, curious to see where he was going.

Sometimes the best thing to do with Rochester is for me to trust his instincts. I wasn't surprised when we ended up at the house a few blocks from us, the place that Joey and Mark had bought the year before.

Mark opened the door before I rang the bell. He was still in his work clothes, a polo shirt and a pair of khakis, but his usual neat appearance was rumpled. His shirt was only half-way tucked in and one of his shoes was untied. "Steve? I've been hoping you'd come by. Is Joey... is he still at the station?"

Before I answered, Rochester pushed past ~~him~~ and bounded up the stairs, his nails clicking on the hardwood floor above. A moment later, he rushed back down, barking insistently.

"Brody's not here, boy," Mark said, his voice tight with worry. "Come in. I closed the shop when Joey called to tell me Rick Stemper wanted him to talk to him. Can I get you some coffee? I've been making pot after pot, to have something to do."

I left the t-shirt on the hall table and followed him into their kitchen, which was all gleaming granite and stainless steel. Mark was the cook in their relationship; Joey could barely make toast.

Mark poured a cup of coffee for me, and one for himself, and we sat at the kitchen table. Rochester slumped down beside me.

"Joey told me about Melissa," Mark said quietly. "He's pretty shaken up. I was still asleep when he got home from his run, but when I woke up..." He paused. "I've never seen him like this."

"Did you know her?"

Mark shook his head. "Joey never mentioned her until he started talking about taking Brody for training. But something wasn't right this morning. I was in the shower when Rick called, but when I came out, I heard Joey crying."

I must have looked surprised, because Mark continued, "Joey never cries. He's not that kind of guy. I was very worried."

Rochester barked, jumped up, and raced to the front door. A moment later, we heard Joey's truck in the driveway, and then he came in with Brody. He unleashed the dog, who raced over to Rochester and went into the play position. But Rochester ignored the pup, focused on the humans.

"I guess I owe you both an explanation," Mark said, dropping heavily into a kitchen chair. Rochester moved to his side, resting his head on Joey's knee. Brody sprawled on the floor beside my dog, white against gold.

"Melissa and I..." He looked at Mark, who nodded encouragingly. "We dated in college. It was sophomore year, and I was... I was trying to figure things out. About myself. About whether maybe I was bisexual instead of just gay."

I remembered the yearbook photo I'd found of the two of them at the Pre-Vet Club fundraiser, looking so young and happy.

"We were together for about six months," Joey continued. "But I knew it wasn't right. When I told her I was more attracted to men, that I wanted to break up... she didn't take it well. She said I'd led her on, used her."

"That was years ago," Mark said softly. "Why didn't you tell me?"

"Because I was ashamed. Not of being bi. I worked through that a long time ago. But I wasn't happy about how I handled things with Melissa. I was young and confused, and I hurt her." Joey's voice cracked. "When I found out she was training dogs here in Stewart's Crossing, I thought maybe... maybe we could clear the air. That's one reason I signed up for sessions with Brody. And I thought she really could help him."

"But she refunded your money," I said.

Joey nodded. "She recognized my name on the registration form. Sent me an email saying she didn't want to work with me, that there was too much history." He looked at Mark. "That's why I was at the park early this morning. I wanted to talk to her before the training clinic and apologize again. To tell her I'd been lost, and I regretted hurting her. But I couldn't find her, even though her car was there."

Rochester whined softly, his tail thumping against the floor. I knew that sound – he'd found what he was looking for, even if I wasn't sure what it was yet.

"Joey," I said carefully, "why didn't you tell Rick about knowing Melissa from Penn State?"

"Because I knew how it would look. I'd be the gay ex-boyfriend who shows up early on the morning she dies? Not a good idea." He shook his head. "I panicked."

He stared down at the dogs and then back at us. "Steve? Mark? I swear, even though her SUV was there, I never saw her. You have to believe me, Mark. Please say you do."

Mark nodded slowly. He reached for Joey's hand. With that added emotional support, Joey turned to me. "Steve, you can help me, can't you? You've worked with Rick before. You've helped him find the person responsible for a crime. You can do that for me, can't you?"

There was an edge of desperation in his voice. I stared at Mark, who was frozen with anguish on his face, and then I turned to Joey, who looked as miserable as I've ever seen.

Joey.

He'd been my friend and co-manager for years, and I thought that I knew him as well as anyone. He wasn't Melissa's killer.

I would do whatever I could to prove that.

5. NEIGHBORHOOD WATCH

Rochester and I took the long way home from Joey and Mark's house, cutting through River Bend's winding paths. I needed time to think about what Joey had told us. Rochester was content to stop and sniff every bush and blade of grass along the way.

We were passing the community mailbox cluster when I heard someone calling my name. Rebecca Patterson, our neighborhood's unofficial news service, was struggling with her standard poodle puppy, Bonaparte. The black pup was attempting to eat his own leash while Rebecca tried to check her mail.

"Steve! Oh thank goodness. Can you hold him for a moment?" She thrust Bonaparte's leash at me before I could answer. "He's going through a phase where everything is either food or a toy. The trainer says it's normal, but honestly..."

While the puppy bounced around him, Rochester sat calmly and maintained his dignified air of an older dog tolerating youthful nonsense. I watched Rebecca dig through her mailbox, wondering if she knew about Melissa's death yet. Rebecca knew everything about everyone in Stewart's Crossing, especially if it involved dogs.

"I heard about that terrible business at the dog park," she said, answering my unspoken question. "Poor Melissa. Though between you and me, I'm not entirely surprised."

"What do you mean?"

Rebecca lowered her voice, though there was no one else around. "Well, she and David were separated. Had been for months, though they kept it quiet. He moved into that new apartment complex by the train station."

This was news to me. "David?"

"David Bloom. Her husband. Or soon-to-be ex-husband, I should say. Marge. You know Marge, with the three corgis? Her sister lives in the same complex, and she said Melissa and David had a terrible fight right in the parking lot last week." Rebecca finally found whatever she was looking for in her mail and closed the box. "Apparently, he was tired of bankrolling her 'dog obsession,' as he called it."

Bonaparte had given up ~~on~~ eating his leash and was now attempting to engage Rochester in play. My dog gave him one gentle nose bump, then looked at me as if to say, "Can we go home now?"

"Did anyone mention this to the police?" I asked.

"Oh, I'm sure they know. They were arguing outside Primo's last month. David was saying she'd maxed out their credit cards on prototypes for a special dog collar." Sarah shook her head. "He wanted her to get a 'real job' instead of 'playing with dogs all day.' Those were his exact words. Gail from the Chocolate Ear heard the whole thing."

So the David Bloom whose online comments I'd read was Melissa's husband. If he was writing that way about her, the divorce must have been a bitter one. Was that a clue that might lead to discovering who killed her?

"The shame of it is," Rebecca continued, taking Bonaparte's leash back, "she was finally ~~just~~ starting to get her business act together. Marge told me Melissa had a meeting scheduled with possible investors this week. Something about franchising her training methods." She gave the leash a gentle tug as Bonaparte tried to chase a squirrel. "Not that I agreed with those training methods, mind you. But still, to be killed-right when things were looking up..."

Rochester was ready to move on but Rebecca had one final thought.

"You know," she said, tapping a finger to her lips, "David works in finance. Investment banking or something like that. I always wondered if that's how Melissa got her initial clients. All those wealthy people with badly behaved designer dogs? They certainly would need her help."

I made a mental note to tell Rick about the argument. A bitter soon-to-be-ex-husband was certainly someone to look into. "We should get going," I said. "Thanks for the information."

"Any time!"

As Rochester and I walked home, I thought about what Rebecca had said. A failing marriage, financial troubles, and professional rivalries. Melissa's life had been more complicated than I'd realized. The question was: which of these threads had led to her death?

6. THE CHOCOLATE EAR

After hearing Rebecca's gossip about David and Melissa's separation, I decided it was time to get the story straight from the source. Not from David, because I didn't know him, and I'd leave questioning him to Rick. Instead I'd check with Gail, who'd witnessed an argument at the Chocolate Ear. I hurried Rochester home and piled him into my SUV to drive back into downtown Stewart's Crossing.

Range Rovers and Volvo SUVs pulled in and out of parking spots along Main Street as mothers ran their weekend errands. A group of kids on bikes wove between parked cars, enjoying these last warm days before school started. Another peaceful day in the suburbs north of Philadelphia.

Rochester's tail started wagging as soon as we turned onto Main Street. The sun warmed the weathered stone facades of eighteenth-century buildings, their deep windowsills casting sharp shadows across the sidewalk. Modern shops occupied the ground floors, but the upper stories still showed their colonial heritage in wavering glass panes and hand-carved woodwork.

The Chocolate Ear had taken over an old brick house, with

the café on the ground floor and an apartment above, where the owner, Gail Dukowski, had lived until her marriage to Declan Hughes. It was bright and cheery, with framed art deco posters of French food labels hung on yellow walls. A hand-painted sign in the window announced, "Dogs Welcome in the Side Room."

The main cafe looked like a Parisian bistro with tiny round tables and bentwood chairs. In the dog-friendly area the tables were spaced farther apart and each had a hook for securing leash handles, and a water bowl that Gail kept filled throughout the day. I hooked Rochester's leash on our regular table in the corner. He settled into a perfect down-stay, knowing that good behavior was required for his special treats.

I walked ~~over~~ to the Dutch door that led to the café.

"There's my favorite customer!" Gail called out. She was behind a small counter that connected to the main cafe's kitchen. Her blonde hair escaped from its clip as usual. "The usual for both of you?"

I agreed and returned to my seat. A few minutes later, Gail brought over my cafe mocha and a house-made peanut butter biscuit for Rochester. She glanced around the empty room before taking the seat across from me.

"I heard about Melissa," she said quietly. "Rick was in earlier asking about the argument she had here with David."

"Rebecca Patterson mentioned that. Said you were here when it happened?"

"They were right over by the front window." Gail absently straightened the vase of fresh flowers on the table. "David came in first, ordered his usual Americano. He was agitated and kept checking his phone. When Melissa arrived, I could tell it wasn't going to be a friendly chat."

Rochester took his biscuit from me with exaggerated gentleness, his eyes never leaving Gail's face as she spoke.

"David started in about a credit card bill for equipment she'd ordered, special collars or harnesses, I think. He said she was obsessed, that it wasn't healthy." Gail shook her head. "Melissa told him she was done apologizing for taking her work seriously. She said he never supported her dreams, just wanted her to be his 'corporate wife' and give up everything she cared about."

"Did either of them mention her plans to open her own facility?"

"Oh yes. That's what really set him off. He said she was delusional if she thought she was going to compete with established trainers like Patricia Morgan." Gail lowered her voice further. "Then Melissa said something interesting. She said she knew things about Patricia's methods that would shut down Pawsitive Solutions overnight."

Rochester's ears pricked forward at Patricia's name. He'd only eaten half his biscuit, which was unusual for him.

"What kind of things?"

"She didn't say. But David laughed, and it was not a nice laugh, you know? He said Melissa was burning bridges all over town, and soon no one would work with her." Gail stood up as the bell over the main entrance tinkled.

"The strange thing is, David was here Saturday morning with his Yorkie Maxwell, around six-thirty. Sat by the window for almost an hour, drinking coffee and making phone calls. He seemed... nervous. Kept looking out at the street. And Maxwell was very agitated, too."

Gail glanced at the two new customers reading the menu on the wall. "There's something else. Declan heard some things at the Chamber of Commerce meeting last week. David's been desperately trying to get local investors interested in some kind of pet technology company. He cornered Martin Borowski from First Stewart's Crossing Bank in the parking lot, practically begging for a meeting."

"That doesn't sound good," I said.

"Declan said he seemed frantic. David kept saying he needed bridge financing, whatever that means. And he was offering the banker ridiculous terms, way above market rate interest." She lowered her voice further. "Declan also heard he'd been calling every venture capital firm between here and New York, trying to get meetings. But apparently his reputation preceded him. Something about questionable deals at his last firm?"

Rochester had finished his biscuit and was watching the door intently, as if he expected David to return.

"The weird thing is," Gail continued, "when Declan mentioned it to me, I remembered overhearing David on his phone right here about a month ago. He was telling someone that 'the patent would solve everything' and that he needed a little more time. He sounded desperate then too."

She shook her head. "I didn't think much of it back then. But now, with what happened to Melissa..." She trailed off as the two customers stepped up to the register, ready to order.

Gail gave Rochester a concerned look. "Is he feeling okay? He usually inhales those biscuits."

I glanced at my dog, who was now staring intently at the side room's entrance. "He's been a little off since this morning," I said. "Gail, did David mention where he was going when he left yesterday?"

"No, but he was wearing running clothes. Seemed odd, since he's usually in a suit when he comes in." She headed over to the counter to take care of the customers. Calling back over her shoulder, she said, "Let me know if you need anything else."

I sat back, processing everything I'd learned. Melissa had dirt on Patricia. David had been in town early on the morning his estranged wife was killed.

The pieces were there, but they weren't fitting together quite right. I pulled out my phone to text Rick about David's early morning visit to the Chocolate Ear, but before I could, Rochester suddenly stood up, hackles raised.

Through the windows, I spotted a dark blue Mercedes sedan parking across the street. The driver got out, wearing running clothes. Was that Melissa's husband David?

7. THE HUSBAND

I watched the man grab a leash from the Mercedes' back seat. A moment later, a tiny Yorkshire terrier hopped out, its silver and tan coat gleaming in the morning sun. The dog trotted beside his dad with the practiced air of a longtime companion, clearly comfortable with their routine.

Rochester's posture had changed. He was head high, ears forward, completely focused on the café's front door. The bell tinkled as the man entered, the Yorkie prancing at his feet. "Morning, Gail," he called out, his voice carrying the forced cheerfulness people use when they're trying too hard to seem normal. "The usual, please."

"Coming right up, David," Gail said, already starting his Americano. If she was thinking about his argument with Melissa, or even about Melissa's death, her professional demeanor didn't show it.

So that was David Bloom. He didn't look like a man whose wife had been found dead that morning—though it was hard to know what that would look like.

David chose a table by the window, near where Rochester and I sat. Up close, I saw signs of strain around his eyes, a slight tremor in his hands as he looped the Yorkie's leash on the dog hook beside him. He was younger than I'd expected, probably in his mid-thirties, wearing expensive running gear. But it didn't look like it had ever seen actual exercise. The fabric was stiff and the shoes were far too clean.

Rochester watched the Yorkie with unusual intensity. Normally he was great with small dogs, but something about this situation put him on high alert. His ears twitched at every movement David made.

"Here you go," Gail said, setting down David's coffee. "Can I get anything for Maxwell?"

The Yorkie sat perfectly at David's feet, and I had to admit he was beautifully trained. Melissa's influence, no doubt.

"No, he's fine," David said, pulling out his phone. He jabbed at the screen with more force than necessary, before lifting it to his ear. "Come on, pick up," he muttered.

Rochester's tail thumped once against the floor. It was not his usual friendly wag, but something more deliberate. Maxwell turned to look at him, head cocked to one side.

"What do you mean, you can't access the account?" David's voice rose sharply. "I don't care what the lawyer says, I need those papers today." He listened for a moment, his free hand clenching into an empty fist. "No, you listen. We had a deal. If you can't handle this, I'll find someone who can."

Maxwell whined softly, picking up on his owner's tension. But instead of trying to comfort the little dog, David jerked the leash sharply. "Quiet," he snapped.

Rochester let out a low rumble—not quite a growl, but a warning. David glanced our way, really seeing us for the first time. His eyes narrowed as they fixed on my dog.

"I have to go," he said into the phone. "Just get it done." He ended the call and took a long drink of his coffee, but his hand was shaking so badly that some spilled onto the table.

"Your golden," he said suddenly, turning to me. "He was one of Melissa's success stories, wasn't he? I recognize him from the photos on her website."

"No," I said. "Must be another dog. But we were planning to attend her clinic this morning."

David's face twisted. "Right. The clinic." He let out a harsh laugh that made both dogs flinch. "Always another free demo to allegedly attract clients. Another certification, another expensive program for her to take. You know what the last one cost? Fifteen thousand dollars. For what? So she could learn new ways to control animals?"

Maxwell pressed against David's leg, trying to climb into his lap, but David pushed him away. Rochester's muscles tensed beneath his fur. I felt tense, too. I didn't like how this man was bullying his Yorkie.

"Melissa loved those dogs more than anything," David continued, his voice bitter. "More than our marriage, more than our future. Even Maxwell here. She gave him to me as a birthday present, and then she spent a fortune training him 'properly.' As if I couldn't handle a six-pound dog on my own."

I watched David carefully. The man sitting across from me didn't seem to be grieving—he was angry. And scared. His right leg bounced nervously under the table, making Maxwell dance sideways to avoid being kicked. Right. He was doing a terrific job interacting with his six-pound puppy.

"Sounds like you had different priorities," I said carefully.

David's laugh was even harsher this time. "Priorities? She was obsessed. And now—" He cut himself off, draining his coffee cup. "Come on, Maxwell. We're done here."

He stood abruptly, nearly knocking over his chair. Maxwell scrambled to keep up as David yanked the leash, heading for the door. But before they reached it, Rochester stood up and gave one sharp, authoritative bark.

David froze, his hand on the door handle. For a moment, he seemed about to say something. Then he pushed through and was gone, practically dragging Maxwell to his car.

I watched through the window as he peeled out of his parking spot, the Mercedes' engine roaring. Maxwell's little face was barely visible in the passenger window.

"You okay, boy?" I asked Rochester, who was still staring at the door. He turned to look at me, and I saw the same certainty in his eyes that I'd seen at the crime scene. David might not have killed Melissa, but I was sure he was involved in some way.

I pulled out my phone to text Rick about David's suspicious behavior and his angry phone call. The pieces were coming together, and I didn't like the picture they were forming. David's financial motives, Patricia's professional rivalry, Joey's complicated history with Melissa. But which one of them had killed her?

Rochester seemed to be asking the same question. He kept looking from the door to me and back again, as if trying to tell me something important. And I'd learned long ago to trust my dog's instincts.

8. PAWSITIVE SOLUTIONS

I decided to take a more direct approach to investigating Melissa's death. If Patricia Morgan had been at the dog park that morning, I wanted to see her reaction when I mentioned Melissa's name. And what better way to do that than to inquire about training for Rochester?

As I'd seen in the photos that accompanied the map location, Pawsitive Solutions occupied an old Victorian on the outskirts of Stewart's Crossing. Close examination showed the wrap-around porch had been enclosed to create a climate-controlled space. I got a better look at the training areas that had been fenced off in the front and side yards.

As soon as I pulled into the parking lot, Rochester's demeanor changed. Usually eager to explore new places, he pressed against the back of my seat, refusing to jump out when I opened the car door.

"Come on, boy. Let's check this place out."

He finally emerged, but he stayed close to my leg as we approached the front door. A bell tinkled as we entered. The reception area smelled strongly of lavender, probably some kind of calming spray for anxious dogs.

A woman appeared with a treat pouch clipped to her belt. She was barely over five feet with close-cropped gray hair and wire-rimmed glasses. Thanks to the open door, I could see into the office. Framed by a window over the desk was a blue Prius.

"Hi, I'm Patricia. Welcome to Pawsitive Solutions!" Her smile faltered slightly as she looked at Rochester. "Is your golden having behavioral issues?"

"Rochester isn't exactly having behavior issues. But he's been acting out a little. I'd planned to take him to Melissa Kawamoto for a tune up. But that's off. I'm sure you've heard the news?"

Patricia's face tightened almost imperceptibly. "Terrible thing. But you know what they say. As you train, so shall you reap."

Rochester's hackles rose slightly. His leash strained as he tried to back away from Patricia.

"I heard the two of you had very different approaches to training," I said carefully.

"Melissa believed in dominating dogs into submission."

Patricia pulled a clicker from her treat pouch. "We use science-based methods here. No force, no fear." She clicked once and held out a treat, but Rochester turned his head away. "That's unusual. Most dogs love our organic chicken treats."

"He's not very food motivated," I lied. Rochester would normally do backflips for chicken, but something about this place had him completely shut down.

Patricia slid the treat back into her pouch. "Melissa and I had our professional disagreements," she continued, her voice tight with frustration. "She criticized my methods publicly, called them outdated. Said treat-based training created fat, dependent dogs." She shook her head. "I've been doing this for thirty years. My clients trust me. Their dogs love me. But Melissa wanted to revolutionize everything with her pressure-point collars and scientific theories."

Her tone was bitter but not threatening, merely the wounded pride of an experienced professional facing a younger challenger. "I wish she'd been willing to collaborate instead of trying to tear down everything I've built."

Turning back to Rochester, Patricia said, "Let's see how he does in our evaluation space." She led us to the enclosed porch. Training equipment was arranged around the room: platforms of various heights, tunnels, and weave poles. "We'll start with some basic behaviors. Does he know 'sit'?"

I gave Rochester the hand signal, and he sat immediately. But he kept his body angled away from Patricia.

She clicked and offered a different treat. Again, he refused it. "Interesting. Does he usually ignore food rewards?"

"He's not always good with strangers," I said, though that wasn't the case at all. "Can I try?"

She handed me the clicker and the treat. "Rochester, lay down," I said.

He stared up at me.

I repeated the command with my hand flat in the air and then moved it down. He looked at me once more, but he went ~~down~~ to the floor. "Good boy," I said. I clicked and then handed him the treat, which he wolfed down.

"Hmm." She made notes on a tablet. "Some dogs need time to acclimate to new environments. We could start with private sessions, before working up to our group classes. Though I should mention, we're quite selective about our clients. We wouldn't want any pets with aggressive tendencies to influence our other dogs."

She totally misread him. Rochester wasn't being aggressive; he was being wary. There's a difference, and any good trainer should know that.

"What exactly happened between you and Melissa?" I asked.

Patricia's smile became brittle. "Creative differences. She

wanted to expand into protection training, attack dog work. I prefer to focus on companion animals." She paused. "Did you know she was planning to open her own facility? Right here in Stewart's Crossing. Though our methods were different, she would have undercut my prices and stolen my clients."

Rochester had moved to the far end of the porch, as far from Patricia as his leash would allow. When she took a step toward him, he gave a low warning rumble, something I'd never heard from him before. She stopped in her tracks.

"Perhaps your dog needs more remedial work than I thought," Patricia said. "Aggression like that needs to be addressed immediately."

"He's not aggressive," I said. "He's telling us something."

Rochester's eyes tracked Patricia's movements. He barely blinked. All his muscles were tense. Whatever he was picking up, it wasn't fear, it was distrust.

"Dogs can't tell us anything except what we've trained them to communicate," Patricia said dismissively. "That's science. Everything else is anthropomorphizing."

I'd heard enough. "I think we'll hold off on training for now. But I appreciate your time."

Back in the car, Rochester immediately relaxed, letting out a long breath. I sat there in the driver's seat for a moment, not moving but thinking about his reaction. I couldn't get past Patricia's dismissive attitude and that crazy comment about reaping what you "train." Who trained a pet to become a killer?

My phone buzzed with a text from Rick: "Got the lab results from the charm bracelet. Traces of lavender oil on the broken chain."

I stared at Patricia's building. Lavender. The same scent that had filled the reception area. Suddenly, Rochester's behavior made perfect sense. He hadn't been reacting to Patricia. He'd recognized a scent from the crime scene.

The question was: what had Patricia Morgan been doing at the dog park at six in the morning? And why hadn't she mentioned being there when she talked about Melissa's death?

9. BEST IN SHOW

The theme song for *Hawaii Five-O* played on my phone right as Lili and I were finishing dinner on Saturday. Rochester, who had been dozing in his bed in the corner, lifted his head at the familiar sound of Rick's ringtone.

"I need a favor tomorrow," Rick said when I answered. "There's a regional dog show in Doylestown. I want to check it out, but I need cover."

"Why not bring Rascal?" I asked. Rick's Australian Shepherd would be at home in such a setting.

"Because I need to focus on conversations, not keeping Rascal from challenging every other male dog there for dominance." Rick paused. "Rochester's better socialized. And you're better at getting people to talk."

Lili had been showing me photos from her morning shoot on her laptop. Now she closed it and raised an eyebrow questioningly.

"Hold on," I said to Rick. To Lili, I explained, "Rick wants us to go to a dog show in Doylestown tomorrow. Apparently, it's relevant to Melissa's case."

"I could get some great shots," she said thoughtfully. "Dog

shows make for amazing photographs. All those handlers trying to keep their dogs perfect while the dogs just want to be dogs."

"Lili wants to come and take pictures," I told Rick. "That would make our cover even better."

"Perfect," Rick said. "The more we look like casual spectators, the better. Meet me there at nine?"

"Sure. Did you ever speak with Patricia Morgan?"

"I interviewed her this afternoon," Rick said. "She claims she always parks near the dog park when she goes to Primo's Bakery for their fresh morning pastries. Says she's done it for years because the bakery's lot is too small. She was there at six because she needed to pick up a special order for a client event."

"Did the bakery confirm it?"

"Yeah, they had her order in their system, two dozen assorted pastries. But here's the thing. She didn't pick the goodies up until seven-thirty. That's a long time to wait in a parked car."

"Did she explain the wait?"

"Said she was reviewing training schedules on her phone and lost track of time. But her phone records show she made three calls during that period, all to the same number. We're tracing it."

After I hung up, Lili opened her laptop again. "Look at this," she said, turning it toward me. "This was the last photo session I did with Melissa."

The image showed Melissa working with a German Shepherd, demonstrating a perfect heel. The dog's eyes were fixed on her face with complete focus.

"She really knew what she was doing," Lili said softly. "Whatever people thought about her methods, she got incredible results."

Leaving his bed, Rochester came over to rest his head on my knee, his usual signal that he needed his evening walk. The streets of River Bend were quiet as we made our circuit. I used the time to think about everything we'd learned.

Patricia Morgan had been at the dog park that morning, but she hadn't admitted it. Not to me, at least. She and Melissa had a professional rivalry that went beyond simple competition. Joey had hidden his past relationship with Melissa, making himself look suspicious. David, Melissa's husband, seemed more angry than grief-stricken about his wife's death.

Rochester had reacted differently to each of them: wary of Patricia, concerned about Joey, and alert to something off about David. My dog's instincts were usually good, but in this case, they were pointing in a variety of directions. But which person was Rochester's pick for the killer?

Then there were those threatening posts on the dog training website, sent from the library's computers. Anyone could have written those comments. Not just the three people I most suspected. It could have been Patricia trying to intimidate a rival, David venting his frustration, or even a disgruntled client.

And then finally, someone had followed through on those threats.

The dog show tomorrow might give us answers. The dog training community was small and tight-knit; someone there might know about the tensions between Melissa and Patricia, or about David's reputation among dog people. If Patricia was there handling client dogs as I assumed she would be, we might learn something about her training methods. I might be able to see what it was that Melissa had found concerning.

The next morning dawned clear and crisp, perfect weather for an outdoor event. Rochester and I took our usual walk, though I kept it shorter than normal, knowing we had a busy day ahead.

The Bucks County Kennel Club held their shows at a large park just outside Doylestown. As we pulled into the parking lot,

I saw dozens of RVs and vans with professional logos, and pop-up tents dotting the grounds. Handlers rushed between rings with perfectly groomed dogs, while spectators wandered among vendor booths selling everything from treats to rhinestone collars.

Rick was waiting by the entrance, in khakis, but without his regular SCPD polo shirt. "The golden retriever ring is over there," he said, pointing. "But I'm more interested in the vendor area. Melissa bought most of her training equipment from these suppliers. Maybe one of them knows something we don't."

Lili already had her camera out, capturing candid shots of nervous handlers making last-minute adjustments to their dogs' coats. Rochester walked calmly beside me, ignoring the excitement around him.

"Steve!" A familiar voice called out. "I didn't know you showed Rochester!"

Sarah Ramsey was struggling toward us. Cocoa was straining at his leash. The chocolate Lab was wearing his prong collar again, but it didn't seem to be having much effect.

"We're spectating," I said. "Are you competing?"

"No, shopping for a new trainer." She looked around nervously. "I heard Patricia Morgan might be here. After what happened to Melissa..." She let the sentence trail off as Cocoa lunged toward a passing Pomeranian.

"Is Patricia showing today?" Rick asked casually.

"She usually handles some client dogs in the obedience trials," Sarah said. "Though I haven't seen her yet. Oh! There's Madge from my puppy class. Excuse me!"

She hurried off, Cocoa dragging her toward a woman with a beautiful but clearly anxious Standard Poodle.

"Interesting," Rick murmured. "Let's check out the obedience rings."

We worked our way through the crowd, stopping occasionally so Lili could take photos. Rochester drew admiring glances from several golden retriever breeders, and I found myself drawn into conversations about bloodlines and conformation.

"Your boy has lovely structure," one breeder told me, running an expert eye over Rochester. "And such a calm temperament. Who did you train with?"

"I was thinking of working with Patricia Morgan," I said. "Do you know her?"

The breeder's face tightened slightly. "I wouldn't," she said quietly. "Some of us have... concerns about her methods. Melissa Kawamoto was gathering evidence." She stopped abruptly, noticing Rick's attention. "I should get back to my dogs. Good luck with your training decisions."

We moved on, but Rochester suddenly stiffened and turned his head. Through the crowd, I caught a glimpse of Patricia's blue Prius pulling into the parking lot.

"Rick," I started to say, but as he moved in that direction, he said, "Stay here. Keep talking to people. I want to see what she does when she thinks no one's watching."

Lili squeezed my arm and lifted her camera. "I'll get some shots of the obedience trials," she said. "Maybe that's tell us what Melissa was so concerned about."

Rochester and I continued our circuit of the show grounds. However, his attention kept returning to the obedience rings. Whatever was going on with Patricia Morgan, my dog seemed determined not to let it go unnoticed.

10. OBEDIENCE TRIALS

Rochester's hackles rose slightly. Following his gaze, I saw David Bloom's Mercedes pulling into the parking lot. Lili and I continued wending our way through the show with Rochester. Our progress was stopped occasionally so people could admire my dog.

Through the crowd, I spotted David moving between vendor booths, carrying a sleek black briefcase. Maxwell wasn't with him this time. David paused when he got to a booth selling training equipment, speaking quietly with the vendor while pulling something from his case. It looked like several identical collars, matte black with a distinctive curved clasp.

The vendor examined one, nodding as David pointed out features. I was too far away to hear their conversation, but their body language suggested a serious business discussion rather than casual shopping.

Commotion from the obedience ring drew our attention. A German Shepherd had broken away from its stay position, dragging its handler, a tall woman in a blue pant suit, toward the spectators. The handler struggled to regain control while judges shook their heads and made notes.

"That's Cherisse Mitchell and Thor," a woman near us whispered to her friend. "Patricia Morgan was training Thor until Cherisse decided Melissa Kawamoto could do a better job."

"Guess she was wrong about that," her friend said.

Rick materialized at my side. "The dog's wearing one of those special collars Melissa was developing," he said quietly. "Look who's watching."

Following his gaze, I spotted Patricia Morgan standing in the shadow of a vendor tent, arms crossed, a satisfied smile on her face as she watched Thor's disqualification.

I also noticed David Bloom pay attention to the commotion. When he saw Cherisse struggling with her dog, his face darkened. He must have recognized the unique collar Thor was wearing. David quickly packed the prototypes back into his briefcase, shaking his head at whatever the vendor was saying.

Rochester watched intently as David hurried toward the parking lot, his phone already at his ear. The same urgency I'd seen at the Chocolate Ear was evident in his stride. This was a man who was desperate for control.

"The timing's interesting," Rick said. "Cherisse's dog acts up while wearing Melissa's design, and simultaneously, David's showing off what looks to me like newer versions of the same collar."

"Almost like he knew there'd be a demonstration of why Melissa's version couldn't be trusted," I said.

"Interesting timing," Rick murmured. "Let's talk to Cherisse."

We found her in the warm-up area, the German Shepherd sitting calm at her side. Her eyes widened when Rick showed his badge.

"I should have stuck with Patricia's methods," she said bitterly, unclipping what the dog's bright orange nylon collar. "Melissa promised me this new design would be revolutionary.

Said it was humane but effective." She handed it to Rick. "Instead, it failed completely. Now I've lost my chance at certification this year."

"May I?" I asked, and Rick passed the collar to me. It looked normal, but the inside had an unusual texture.

"It's supposed to provide better feedback without force," Cherisse explained. "But something spooked Thor while he was in the stay position. It was like he suddenly got an electric shock, even though that's impossible. Melissa promised these were completely mechanical."

Rick took the collar from me. "I'd like to have this examined, if you don't mind."

"I don't mind," Cherisse said. She seemed completely defeated.

"Did Melissa explain how this worked?"

"Something about bio-feedback sensors that detect muscle tension, heart rate, or other signs of stress or aggression before the dog actually acts out," she said. "She was very secretive about the actual mechanics. Said she was worried about patent issues."

She patted Thor's head. "The strange thing is, Patricia came by last week asking lots of questions about how the collar worked and if it was successful. I didn't want to betray Melissa, so I said very little." She gestured at the obedience ring. "Maybe I should have given up then and gone back to Patricia."

As we walked away, Rick held up the collar. "It takes a lot of money to bring a new product to market. Sounds like that was the source of the problems between Melissa and her husband."

"In part. He complained about a lot of her charges. And he downplayed her likelihood of success. She needed funding for patents and manufacturing, and those were only the parts I heard," I said. "But think about it. "There was a reason Melissa persisted with her quest. These collars must have shown promise. Don't forget, they seem advanced enough to make Patricia nervous. She was even interested enough to spy on her former employee!"

Rochester watched the German Shepherd and handler leave, his expression thoughtful. I'd seen that look before, usually when he knew something important but couldn't tell me what it was.

"I'm having this analyzed," Rick said, bagging the collar. "But Steve? Be careful what equipment you let people put on Rochester. Someone at this show knows more than they're telling about Melissa's death. And they might not want her methods examined too closely."

11. FOLLOW THE MONEY

A separate channel of the Delaware bordered River Road north of Stewart's Crossing. It was a delightful spot where the river was broad and placid. Rochester loved to watch the fields and housing developments go by from the car window, and that Monday morning it was cool enough to roll it down. He loved sticking his head out into the summer air.

Friar Lake, the conference center I ran for Eastern College, was an impressive property. It boasted a Gothic-style chapel, a cluster of dormitories, and a handful of other buildings built of native fieldstone. Its hilltop location provided a vista of fields and forests down to the Delaware River.

Joey's truck was already in his usual spot when I reached my office. I found a note from him saying he would be out on the property, supervising the college maintenance workers who came regularly to mow the lawns and tidy the flower beds.

Rochester settled into his bed in the corner of my office while I tackled the usual Monday morning flood of emails. But I couldn't focus. The contrast between Joey's obvious distress, Patricia's cavalier indictment of Melissa's training efforts, and

David's barely concealed anger kept nagging at me. My eyes kept returning to my hacker laptop, which I had brought with me that morning.

A knock at my door made Rochester's tail thump against the floor. Joey stood in the doorway, and it was clear he hadn't slept well. His usual neat appearance was rumpled, and dark circles shadowed his eyes.

"Got a minute?" he asked.

"Of course." I gestured to the chair across from my desk. "How are you holding up?"

"Not great." He sank into the chair. "Mark's worried sick, I can barely focus on work, and Rick Stemper probably thinks I killed my college girlfriend." He ran a hand through his disheveled hair. "The worst part is, I keep thinking if I'd only been honest from the start about knowing Melissa..."

Rochester got up and moved to Joey's side, resting his head on my friend's knee. Joey absently scratched behind his ears.

"I saw Melissa's husband Saturday," I said. "At the Chocolate Ear. He didn't exactly seem broken up about her death. And then yesterday, I was at the big dog show in Doylestown. David Bloom was there, too, and he looked like he was trying to sell a new version of the collar Melissa created."

Joey looked up sharply. "David was always jealous of how much time she spent with her clients' dogs. He bought this expensive trip to Hawaii for their fifth anniversary, but she cut it short because a client's dog was having anxiety issues." He shook his head. "He made sure she paid for that decision for months."

"You talked to her? I thought you were estranged since you broke up with her in college."

He wiggle-waggled a hand in the air. "It was awkward. But when we ran into each other last year at the IGA market, we connected again as friends. When she realized I was living in

Stewart's Crossing, Melissa started coming by the antique store on days when she saw my truck outside." He absently petted Rochester.

"At first it was casual conversation, but after a while, she started opening up about David. How he was pressuring her to give up her business, how he'd get angry when she spent their money on training equipment. She told me things she probably hadn't told anyone else, about the prototype collars she was developing, about how David insisted on taking control of their accounts."

He paused, running a hand through his hair. "I think she felt safe talking to me because of our history. She knew I understood her passion for working with dogs. It's what attracted me to her in college, when I was still figuring myself out. Maybe she thought that because I was gay, I didn't have any stake in their marriage politics."

"But something changed?"

"Yeah. Last week, she came by the shop, looking really upset. Said David had threatened to contest the patent rights to her collar design. She'd been venting about their fights, showing me her documentation. Then suddenly she got this look on her face, like she realized how much she'd revealed. The next day, she refunded my training fees and said she couldn't work with Brody anymore." He looked down at his hands. "I think she was worried I might be called as a witness if things got ugly with David. I knew too much about their finances, their fights... about how scared she was getting."

"I've heard that sometimes women are more comfortable confiding their marital problems to their gay male friends," I said.

"Mark is the worst," Joey said, with a hint of a smile. "Every straight female customer always has gossip for him, either about their own husbands or someone else's."

His phone buzzed with a text. "Crap. One of the lawnmowers ran into a ditch. I'd better get out there." After Joey left, I pulled out my hacker laptop. Time to see what I could learn about Melissa's business dealings.

Her company, Alpha Dog Training LLC, had been in business for a long time, registered at the address she shared with David Bloom. Six months ago, she had switched the address to a box at the local pack and ship company. That wasn't unusual in itself; often as a small business grows, it needs a business address. But I wondered if it was related to her divorce proceedings.

I closed the financial records and opened a new browser window. Patent searches hadn't revealed anything. Either Melissa hadn't filed yet, or she was still in the confidential provisional phase. But there might be another way to find out what she'd been developing.

Rochester watched from his bed as I pulled up Google's login page. Had Melissa had been organized enough to keep information in her email box? I knew a lot of people who used the Gmail service, so I started there.

First try: MKawamoto@gmail.com. Email confirmed. Now for the password.

I considered what I knew about Melissa. Penn State grad, class of 2005. Dog trainer. The German Shepherd in her website photos. I tried combinations:

NittanyLions2005 - No

PennState05 - No

TrainerK9 - No

I looked at Rochester, who was sitting up, alert, in a pose captured by Lili in one of my favorite photos. I smiled at Rochester, remembering that photo, and he barked once.

Then I remembered the yearbook photo of Melissa with her

German Shepherd puppy. What was a vet student likely to name her first dog?

Hippocrates2005

I was able to log into her Google account. There were files stored in her Google Drive.

"Got it, boy," I said to Rochester, who lifted his paw at my tone. I reached over and grabbed his paw and shook it.

Melissa's drive was meticulously organized. Folders for client records, training plans, business documents. One was labeled "Project Guardian."

Inside, I found technical drawings, testing videos, and a document titled "Final Specifications." The collar design was innovative: instead of using shock or spray deterrents, it employed a system of carefully calibrated pressure points based on canine acupressure. When activated by sounds or muscle tension indicating stress or aggression, it would apply gentle, precise pressure to calm the dog.

The notes showed months of testing, refining pressure locations and intensities. This wasn't just a training tool. It was a completely new approach to managing dog behavior. If it worked, it would be worth millions.

A subfolder labeled "Legal" contained correspondence with patent attorneys. The most recent email was from an attorney and dated three days before her death:

"Melissa: David's attorneys are contesting the sole inventor status on your patent application. They claim his financial contribution entitles him to joint ownership. Strongly recommend you document all development work done after separation."

Another folder held video clips of prototype testing. The first few showed dogs responding well to the collar, calming quickly when it was activated. But the last video, called Thor-Cherisse, was different. A German Shepherd, the same one from the obedience trial, was wearing what looked like an identical collar. However, instead of being calmed, the animal reacted with panic, as if receiving a shock.

The video filename included yesterday's date. That told me someone had accessed this drive after Melissa's death. But who?

Rochester came over and rested his head on my knee, but his attention was focused on the screen where the German Shepherd was still frantically trying to escape the collar. My dog had seen something in that video that I hadn't yet understood. One thing was clear. Melissa's invention could either revolutionize dog training or be twisted into something much darker.

12. CHARMED

My phone buzzed with a text from Joey. "Bad headache. Going home early. Can you lock up?"

That was unusual. Joey was normally very healthy. Was his headache the result of worry over Melissa's death? Or Rick's suspicion that he was involved with Melissa's death? I responded with a thumbs-up emoji as well as the animated smiley face that implied "take care."

I logged out of Melissa's account and shut down the hacker laptop. I cleaned up a few outstanding items. Then it was time to take Rochester for a walk around the property where we'd make sure all the doors were locked and any equipment put away.

I didn't usually put him on a leash when there were no guests on the property, because I trusted him to come to me when called. I walked from the chapel to the dormitories to the refectory, which we used as a kitchen-slash-dining hall. When I was ready to head back to my office in the gatehouse, I called to Rochester.

He didn't answer, so I tried again. "Rochester! Here, boy!"

He barked several times in quick succession, and I followed the sound. He was far down the property by the old stone building that Joey used as an office and workshop. This was where he regularly repaired our equipment, as well as keeping records of orders and maintenance services.

Rochester was sitting on his haunches. "What's up, boy?" I asked.

He barked once more, and I walked over to him. Then he slumped to the ground, all four of his legs beneath him, and rested his head on the grass.

I squatted down beside him and stroked the soft golden hair on his head. He sniffed twice, and I looked in the direction he was facing. The afternoon sunlight glinted off something gold. I went over to check out the glimmer. A tiny circle engraved with the words "good dog" was peeking out of the grass.

Well, that certainly applied to Rochester, who was a very good dog. But what was it doing out there, near Joey's office? Joey wasn't the type to wear a charm bracelet.

But Melissa Kawamoto was. Had she come out to Friar Lake to speak with Joey at some point and lost her charm?

Of course, it was entirely possible she'd been here. Periodically, I had to head to the Eastern campus in Leighville for meetings or I met with Lili for lunch. Those brief absences would leave Joey on his own on the property. But why hadn't he mentioned it, either to me or to Rick?

It was curious and troubling. I always kept clean tissues in my back pocket, usually to wipe drool from Rochester's mouth. Using one now, I wrapped the tiny charm in it.

On the way home, I debated what to do with what I'd found. Take it to Rick? Maybe. But I had no real reason to believe it was Melissa's. Showing it to him might direct more suspicion to Joey with no reason.

When I came to Ferry Road, I turned inland to River Bend. I was ready to make the turn to Sarajevo Way, when Rochester put his paw on my knee. That was enough reason for me to continue straight ahead to the house that Joey and Mark shared.

Their model came with a single-car garage and a driveway wide enough for two vehicles. However, Joey had long ago commandeered the garage as a workshop, so both his truck and Mark's van were parked there. I drove down the street to the guest parking area and put Rochester on his leash before opening the car door.

"No mischief," I warned him, as he jumped out behind me.

As we walked up the driveway between the two vehicles, Brody began barking from inside the house, and Rochester responded.

"The canine chorus," I said.

Mark opened the front door, blocking Brody from squeezing between his legs. "Hey, Steve, what's up?"

"Can I talk to Joey?"

"He took some pills and went to sleep. Can I help you with something?"

I pulled the tissue from my pocket. "Recognize this?"

"My charm!" he said. "I've been missing that. Come on inside."

His charm? Not Melissa's? I hadn't noticed Mark wearing a charm bracelet either.

Brody took off in a circuit around the downstairs, and I unhooked Rochester's leash so he could follow. Mark led me to the kitchen, where he pulled a keychain from the counter. "Mark bought me this a few months ago," he said, holding it up.

The end of the chain was a tiny metal sculpture of a golden retriever. A chain of about three inches led to a key ring with a bunch of keys on it. Several tiny trinkets relating to dogs were attached with metal jump rings. A dog dish, a bone, a pawprint. There was an empty space between the pawprint and a tiny doghouse.

"I know it's silly, but I love this keychain," Mark said. "I didn't realize I'd lost this one for a few days so I had no idea where to look." He took the charm from me. "I'll have to get Joey to solder it again. Where did you find it?"

The dogs gave up racing and flopped in a pile beside us.

"Outside Joey's office."

Mark tilted his head in confusion. "I haven't been to Friar Lake in ages." Then something occurred to him. "Joey accidentally took my keys with him to work one day about a week ago. That's when it must have happened."

He showed me the keys. "The only ones on here are the house keys, and fortunately that day I was able to lock up with our spare key."

"Well, I'm glad I was able to find it." I reached down and hooked Rochester's leash again. "I hope Joey feels better."

"I hope so too. This whole situation has him very upset."

I was glad that the "good dog" charm hadn't implicated Joey in Melissa's death, and I was troubled that I'd been so quick to suspect him. In fact, I was so caught up in those thoughts that I totally forgot that I had parked in the guest area until we were nearly home. Two houses away, I realized my mistake. At that point, I decided to leave my car in the guest parking area until later.

Lili had a dinner date with her friend Gracious Chigwe, so I fixed myself a bowl of pasta and poured chow for Rochester. Then I settled at the dining room table with my hacker laptop to continue looking into what might have caused Melissa's death. But where to start? David's financial dealings? Patricia's training records? The threatening posts?

Rochester's sudden bark startled me from my thoughts. He stood at the sliding glass doors, watching a woman walking a Yorkshire Terrier past our house.

Something about the little dog caught his attention. That

wasn't his usual reaction to neighborhood pets. Then I remembered: David Bloom's Maxwell.

Was Rochester demanding I pay more attention to the relationship between David and Melissa? What had prompted her to give him a dog he hadn't even wanted? In fact, I didn't know very much about him at all, other than he was a money guy.

I started digging deeper into David's background. Perhaps there was something there that would move him out of suspicion. Or forward.

13. BUSINESS DEVELOPMENT

LinkedIn showed that David was Managing Director of Consumer Products at Innovative Ventures, a boutique Manhattan investment firm. His profile outlined an impressive path: Wharton undergrad, two years at Goldman Sachs, then Columbia Business School, Class of '05—the same year I got my MA in English. That meant David would have been there while my friend Tor Svenson was getting his MBA.

Although I considered him my oldest friend, I hadn't spoken to Tor for a while. This was the perfect excuse for a call.

"Hello, Steve," he answered, his Swedish accent a bit softer than usual. "How have you been?"

We chatted for a few minutes and he asked, "Solved any crimes lately?" Because I'd asked for his help a few times in the past, he knew about how I occasionally helped Rick.

"I'm working on something now. Do you remember a guy named David Bloom from b-school?"

"Oh, yeah. I took a lot of finance classes with him. He was smart but arrogant. Is he in trouble?"

"Someone killed his soon-to-be ex-wife the other day.

Because I saw that he went to school with you, I thought you could give me some background that might be useful to Rick."

"He was recruited right from Columbia by Goldman Sachs. Started out as an associate, creating pitch books for potential deals. Hold on a second, let me do a quick search."

I heard him at his keyboard. "He made VP after three years, so that would have been 2008," Tor said. "At that stage, he'd have been leading smaller deals. Hold on, here's something."

I waited while he read what he'd found.

"You can take this how you want," Tor said. "And I'm reading between the lines here, but it's giving me the distinct impression he was involved in shaky business deals. The kind that skate right on the edge of regulatory issues. Normally, he would have been promoted to Senior VP after about five or six years, but he didn't make it. He left Goldman for a smaller bank called Innovative Ventures in 2012."

He hummed for a moment. "Wait! That's right. I remember a rumor that he got married somewhere in there, and his wife wanted to raise dogs. That was the reason given for them looking for property out in the country. I think they ended up in Westchester County somewhere."

I heard him take a drink. Probably Scotch on the rocks, if his habit was still the same. "Is he in Stewart's Crossing now?"

"He is. The woman he married became a dog trainer, and they moved here about a year ago to set up her business."

"I'm sorry to hear about his wife," Tor said. "Send him my condolences if you can. And I'll let you know if I hear anything else."

"That would be great. And we have to get together soon. You can bring the kids out one Sunday. Give them a taste of fresh air."

"We have fresh air in Manhattan," he said. "We just have to run air purifiers to get it."

I laughed, and we agreed to text with a couple of possible dates. Then I hung up.

I turned back to my computer and found the website for Innovative Ventures, which featured success stories about bringing inventors' ideas to market. One name kept appearing in the testimonials: Colin Whitaker, former VP of Engineering at PetTech Industries.

Whitaker's own profile revealed several patents for pet training devices. His most recent filing, eighteen months ago, described a "pressure-based behavior modification system." It sounded remarkably similar to Melissa's design. The filing had been abandoned six months later, right around the time Melissa incorporated Alpha Dog Training.

"Well, will you look at this," I said to Rochester, who had been dozing in his bed. I turned my laptop to show him a photo from Whitaker's Facebook page. He stood next to a blue Prius. The caption read: "My new hybrid. Better for the environment and my wallet!"

"Very interesting, huh? Same color and make as Patricia's."

Rochester's ears pricked forward. Both of us remembered the Prius that had been found in the dog park when Melissa was murdered. Which one was it?

I was still browsing at Whitaker's website when Lili came home. "What are you up to now?" she asked, as she came over to the table. She looked at the screen. "Oh! Is that the same Colin Whitaker who lives across the street from Gracious?"

"Hard to imagine there's more than one," I said. I did a quick search and discovered that the inventor lived on Palatial Drive, the same street where Gracious and her husband Edward lived.

"Gracious is always complaining about him," Lili said. "He has five big dogs, all rescues, and he doesn't control them very well. And he also doesn't pick up after them."

That was a cardinal sin in any community, particularly one

controlled by a homeowner's association that had the power to levy fines against those who didn't clean up. "Has the Crossing Estates HOA come after him?"

"Gracious says yes. She was irritated at finding dog poop in her yard, so she had Edward put up security cameras. She caught Whitaker letting his Doberman poop in front of her house and not picking it up." She smiled. "She printed the picture on a piece of heavy stationery and put it in an envelope. Then she handed it to him."

"The picture, not the poop?"

"Exactly. She said the expression on his face was priceless, especially after she told him she was sending a copy to the HOA. He promised to do better."

"And has he?"

"Well, the dogs aren't pooping in her yard, but according to her neighbors, he's moved on to other lawns."

I looked at Rochester, who had that abashed look on his face he gets when he's pooping. That gave me an idea.

14. PALATIAL DRIVE

I called Rick and told him what I'd learned. "I have an idea," I said. "Suppose you go over to his house and say that you're following up on complaints from the HOA. I'll come with you and say that I'm from the fine committee."

"And what does that get us?"

"It gets us into his house, for starters," I said. "If he has five dogs, I'm sure you can find a way to bring Melissa Kawamoto into the conversation. See what he's willing to say about working with her."

"It's six o'clock now," Rick said. "Suppose I pick you up in half an hour?"

"I'll be ready. I'll bring what I have on Whitaker so you can read it before we get there."

I printed up what I'd learned about Whitaker and his patent applications, including his connection to David Bloom. Rochester watched me intently, his tail thumping softly against the floor.

"Sorry, I can't take you with me," I said. "Whitaker has too many dogs of his own, and I don't know how they'll behave."

Rochester began jumping around eagerly when Rick pulled

up in the driveway. I had to push my dog aside with my legs to keep him in the house. He barked as I walked out to Rick's truck.

"You'd better pull out fast, or the dog is going to keep barking," I said.

We drove out to Ferry Street. Rick pulled over on the side of the road to read what I had found. "Interesting connection to Melissa Kawamoto," he said.

"And he lives in Stewart's Crossing, so he has access to the library to send those threatening emails. Plus, he owns a blue Prius, which comes up on the video from the dog park. That one you saw on video could be his if it's not Patricia Morgan's."

"You don't need to remind me of everything, you know," he said. "I am a trained detective. I can figure a few things out myself."

"Sorry. You know I get excited when I discover things."

"Yeah, you and your dog."

The late afternoon sun cast long shadows across Whitaker's driveway where his blue Prius sat. A chaotic symphony of barking announced us as we walked to the front door.

"Down, everyone!" a commanding voice called from inside. The door opened to reveal a man in his fifties. He was shorter than I expected, with thinning gray hair and wire-rimmed glasses that made him look more like an accountant than an engineer. He wore cargo shorts and a polo shirt with grease stains on the sleeves.

Behind him, two German Shepherds, a Rottweiler, a Doberman, and a Belgian Malinois jostled for position.

"Mr. Whitaker?" Rick showed his badge. "Detective Stemper. Mr. Levitan is from the Crossing Estates fine committee. We're following up on complaints about violations of the township's pet waste ordinance."

"Come in," Whitaker said, pulling a clicker from his pocket. With quick successive clicks and firm commands, he directed each dog: "Klaus, place. Hans, corner. Rex, down. Duke, stay. Shadow, heel."

The two German Shepherds moved to separate designated spots: Klaus to a mat by the window, Hans to a corner. The Rottweiler, Rex, dropped into a down position, while the Doberman, Duke, froze in place. The Malinois, Shadow, stuck close to Whitaker's left leg. Each movement was precise and practiced.

"I can't imagine why anyone would complain. I always clean up after them."

Each dog wore a different style collar. The Rottweiler's looked like standard leather, but the others had electronic components.

"The HOA has documented several incidents," Rick said, pulling out his notebook. "Including photos."

"Those could be from any dog," Whitaker protested. The Malinois pressed against his leg, and he absently adjusted its collar. "Besides, I usually let my dogs out in my yard, and it's fenced."

While Rick continued asking about the HOA complaints, I noticed how differently each dog behaved. Klaus and Rex the Rottweiler were calm, but the others seemed anxious, especially when Whitaker raised his voice.

"Well, thanks for your time," Rick said. "We'll look into these complaints further." He handed Whitaker a warning notice. "You might want to document when and where you walk your dogs. Just to protect yourself."

"Your dogs are quite well-behaved," I said, letting the Doberman sniff my hand. "Are those special training collars they're wearing?"

Whitaker's demeanor shifted instantly from defensive to enthusiastic. "Prototypes. Each one tests a different approach." He pointed to the German Shepherds. "Klaus has the original pressure-point design. Hans wears the modified version with enhanced feedback."

Klaus seemed relaxed, but Hans kept shaking his head as if the collar bothered him.

"And the others?" I asked.

"Various iterations. I have a workshop out back, where I tinker with things." Whitaker petted the Malinois. "The basic principle is the same, but the implementation varies. Pressure points, muscle tension sensors, even heart rate monitoring."

Obviously, he was eager to chat with someone about his inventions, because he said, "Would you like to see my workshop?"

Of course, I agreed. Only the Malinois accompanied us through the house and out the back door, where a prefabricated building took up much of the back yard.

The workshop smelled of solder and machine oil. Workbenches lined the walls. These surfaces were covered with electronic components and half-assembled devices. What looked like dog collars in various stages of completion hung from pegboards.

He picked up one of the collars. "This was supposed to be my breakthrough. A humane training device using targeted pressure points. But I made a fundamental mistake in choosing a funding partner."

"David Bloom?" I asked.

He turned sharply toward me. "You know him?"

"He went to business school at Columbia with an old friend of mine," I said. Then I embroidered a bit. "When he moved to Stewart's Crossing, Tor introduced us, and I met him and his wife."

"Melissa Kawamoto," he said, and his hand tightened on the collar. "I knew David through investments he made in my previous employer, so when I struck out on my own and needed funding, I approached him. We talked about money for a while. He introduced me to Melissa last year. Said she had interesting ideas about dog training and he thought we might collaborate."

Rick and I both watched him. He spoke quickly, as if he had a lot to say and needed to get it all out.

"We worked together for months, refining the pressure system and testing prototypes. Then suddenly she stopped returning my calls. Next thing I knew, she'd filed a patent application. My name wasn't on it."

"That must have made you angry," Rick said.

"Of course it did! She took my research and my designs. Said she'd 'modified them significantly' enough to claim sole authorship." He set down the collar carefully. "I tried reasoning with her. Offered to share credit. But she claimed her changes made it a completely different device."

"So you decided to prove her wrong," I said. "By modifying the collars to malfunction during demonstrations."

Whitaker's eyes narrowed. "I would never do anything to hurt a dog. Were you at the dog show in Doylestown?"

"I was," I said. "With my wife and my golden retriever." I thought it best to leave Rick out of it. "Were you there?"

"I was. I've been working with Patricia Morgan, documenting problems with Melissa's design. Patricia thought if we could demonstrate the flaws publicly, it would force Melissa to acknowledge the technical issues." He adjusted his glasses. "But now... I can't believe she's dead. I wanted to discredit her work, not..." He trailed off, hands fidgeting with a collar on his workbench.

"You and Patricia sabotaged the demonstration?" Rick asked.

"Not exactly sabotage. We wanted to show how easily her 'revolutionary' design could malfunction. We modified one of the test collars to prove the point." Whitaker looked down at his hands.

"I wanted to show that without my expertise, Melissa's design was fundamentally flawed. You see, the pressure system could easily be altered to cause pain instead of calm." He gestured at his workbench. "I brought a clicker with me and hit a couple of buttons that activated a sensor on Thor's collar. I didn't expect him to react so strongly."

"Did you expect Melissa to be there?" I asked.

"Yes. She had bragged about using the collar to train Thor, and this was going to be her big demonstration. But I didn't see her there."

"Where were you Saturday morning?" Rick asked.

"Here." But his hand trembled slightly as he adjusted his glasses. "I'd planned to confront her at the training clinic. Show her what happened when someone modified her precious design."

"Was that your Prius at the dog park on Saturday morning?" Rick asked.

Whitaker's hand froze on the Malinois's collar. "No, Rex was having diarrhea, and I didn't want to leave until he felt better. Must have been someone else's car. Lots of people have those blue Priuses. Even Patricia. She bought hers after I got mine."

Before we left, I looked around the workshop one more time. The engineer's obsession with the collar design was obvious. But was it enough to drive him to murder? Or had someone else taken advantage of the confusion around the modified collars to kill Melissa?

Back in Rick's truck, he turned to me. "Did you notice how the dogs reacted when I mentioned Saturday morning?"

"The dogs knew something was wrong," I said. "And those collars. Some calmed them, but others seemed to cause distress."

"We need proof he was at the park that morning. I'll get a warrant to search his workshop and analyze those collars." Rick started the engine. "I think we're getting close to understanding what happened to Melissa."

The question was: what would we find in Whitaker's workshop that could connect him to Melissa's death?

Rick drove me back to River Bend's guest parking area where I'd left my SUV earlier. "Something tells me those collars will give us the evidence we need."

I drove the short distance home, thinking about the anxious dogs and their modified collars. More importantly, I wondered what those collars might reveal about Melissa's death.

15. DIGITAL EYES

Tuesday morning found me at my desk at Friar Lake, reviewing vendor contracts while Rochester dozed in his favorite spot by the window. The conference center was quiet. We had a church group arriving on Thursday, but for now the only sounds were distant lawnmowers and the soft whir of my laptop fan.

Joey hadn't come in yet, which was unusual. He typically arrived before me to coordinate with the maintenance crew. His absence felt important after yesterday's revelations about Whitaker and the collars.

My phone buzzed with a text from Rick: "Need to see you. Coming to Friar Lake."

Twenty minutes later, Rick's truck pulled into the parking lot. Rochester's tail started wagging before Rick even knocked on my office door.

"Got something interesting from the Sunoco station at Ferry and River Road," Rick said, pulling out his phone. "Their security cameras cover part of the lot by the dog park."

He showed me grainy footage timestamped six-seventeen

AM Saturday. Joey's truck was clearly visible pulling into the gas station. "Watch this," Rick said.

The footage showed Joey getting out, going inside the store, and coming back out with coffee and what looked like a breakfast sandwich. The timestamp read six-twenty-two AM.

"So he wasn't at the park when he said he was?"

"Better than that," Rick said. "Look at the time stamp when he finally drives away. Six-forty-five AM. The ME puts time of death between six-fifteen and six-forty-five. Joey physically couldn't have killed Melissa."

"Have you told him?"

"Not yet. Wanted to show you first since you vouched for him." Rick tucked his phone away. "Got to admit, that college girlfriend angle had me worried. But the footage doesn't lie."

Relief flooded through me. "He's cleared?"

"Officially. Though I'd still like to know why he wasn't straight with us about knowing Melissa." Rick glanced at Rochester, who had moved to sit between us. "Your boy seemed sure about Joey's innocence from the start."

"He's got good instincts about people." I thought about how distressed Joey had been over the past few days. "Want me to call him?"

"Actually, I'd rather tell him in person. Any idea where he is?"

Before I could answer, Rochester barked and trotted to the window. Joey's truck was pulling into the lot.

When Joey walked in, his face was drawn and tired. He stopped short seeing Rick. "Detective?"

"Got some good news," Rick said. "Security footage from the Sunoco shows you were there getting breakfast when Melissa was killed. You're officially cleared as a suspect."

Joey sank into a chair, his shoulders sagging with relief. "Thank God." He looked at me. "I should have been honest from the start about knowing her. I just... I didn't want to complicate things given my history with her. I should have told you everything sooner."

"Sometimes trying to simplify things only makes them more complex," I said.

Rochester moved to Joey's side and put his head on my friend's knee. Joey scratched behind his ears. "Where does this leave the investigation?"

"We're looking at a few other angles," Rick said. "Including those prototype collars Melissa was developing."

"The ones David was so angry about?" Joey asked. "Melissa told me he was furious about how much money she was spending on development."

Rick's expression sharpened. "What else did she tell you about the collars?"

"Only that she was close to a breakthrough. Something about using pressure points instead of electronic stimulation." Joey frowned. "She mentioned someone else was working on similar technology, but her approach was completely different."

"Different enough to be worth killing over?" Rick asked.

"You'd have to ask David about that," Joey said. "All I know is Melissa was excited about the potential. She truly believed she could revolutionize dog training."

Rochester's ears pricked forward at David's name. I remembered his reaction to Maxwell the Yorkie at the Chocolate Ear, that mix of concern and alertness.

"Thanks for your patience," Rick said to Joey. "Sorry we had to put you through all of this."

After Rick left, Joey turned to me. "Once again, I really am sorry I wasn't straight with you about Melissa."

"You were trying to protect yourself," I said. "And Mark. I get it."

"Still." He stood up. "I should get to work. The church group's coming Thursday and we've got a lot to do to prepare."

As he headed for the door, Rochester gave a soft woof. Joey turned back. "Thanks for believing in me, boy," he said quietly.

I watched my friend walk across the parking lot to his truck. One suspect cleared, but we were still no closer to understanding what had happened to Melissa that morning at the dog park.

Rochester came back to my desk and rested his chin on my knee, his brown eyes serious. Whatever he knew about David and those collars, I had a feeling we were getting closer to the truth.

I finished a few work emails, including approving several contracts. Then I retrieved my hacker laptop from my messenger bag and turned it on. With one suspect cleared, and what I'd learned from Whitaker, it was time to look more closely at Patricia Morgan's background. Rochester settled back onto the floor while I started digging.

Patricia's website showed she'd been training dogs for over thirty years, starting with hunting dogs and expanding into pet obedience. She'd won multiple awards from kennel clubs and had a long list of testimonials from wealthy clients whose difficult dogs she'd reformed.

But digging deeper revealed some concerns. Several former clients had posted on dog training forums about their pets' weight after working with her. One detailed how their Golden Retriever would no longer obey any commands without getting a food reward, and that had led to obesity.

Others echoed similar complaints. Patricia had responded by saying they were using treats that were too fatty. She had started her own line of low-fat treats, but a problem at the manufacturing company had caused her to shut it down.

The company she contracted with to make her "Pawsitive

Rewards" low-fat treats had a salmonella outbreak in 2013 that sickened several dogs. Though her treats weren't implicated, she immediately pulled her line and canceled her contract. The incident made the local news and cost her nearly $50,000 in lost inventory and legal fees.

The Stewart's Crossing *Boat-Gazette* had profiled her five years ago when she opened Pawsitive Solutions. The article mentioned her "old school" treat-based approach clashing with newer behavioral methods.

I found an industry blog post where Melissa had challenged these methods. Without naming Patricia directly, she criticized trainers who used "outdated food rewards." The post ended with Melissa announcing her plans to publish research on more useful alternatives.

Rochester came over and put his head on my knee, his expression serious. We'd cleared Joey, but the deeper we dug, the more complicated this case became.

16. THOSE WHO CAN'T SPEAK

Later that afternoon Rick called. "Remember how Whitaker claimed he was home with a sick dog on Saturday morning? A neighbor's Ring doorbell caught footage of him at 6:23, wearing pajama bottoms and a T-shirt, walking the Rottweiler. I watched the video, and the dog is moving sluggishly, clearly unwell."

"So he's in the clear?"

"He is. The same camera caught him again at 6:37, and a different neighbor's camera picked him up at 6:45. That means it wasn't his blue Prius at the dog park. Which leaves us with two main suspects."

"David Bloom and Patricia Morgan. And she's the one with the blue Prius."

"Exactly. David Bloom's financials just came in. He's been hemorrhaging money for months. Massive credit card debt, failed investments, and get this: three days before Melissa died, he tried to sell a 'revolutionary' dog training system to PetTech Industries."

Rochester's ears pricked forward at the mention of David's name.

"The same company Whitaker used to work for?"

Rick nodded. "David claimed he had full rights to the technology. But Melissa's patent application would have exposed that lie."

Rochester moved to the window, watching the fields around Friar Lake. His posture was alert but not tense, the same way he'd reacted to Maxwell at the Chocolate Ear.

"So he had motive," I said. "We need to take a closer look at David's attempts to sell those collar designs. And maybe talk to Maxwell's vet about any recent changes in the dog's behavior."

"David Bloom's Yorkie? Why?"

"Because Rochester's been trying to tell us something about that dog since the beginning. And I've learned to trust his instincts."

After I hung up with Rick, I pulled out my hacker laptop and did a deep dive into David Bloom's financial situation, and I found evidence of multiple failed investments, margin calls, credit card debt in the high six figures. The kind of trouble that makes people desperate.

Further digging revealed that David took out loans using the potential patent revenues as collateral. In material I found online, he promised investors he had full rights to the technology. If Melissa divorced him before the patent was approved, he'd get nothing, and those investors would come calling. He needed to own that patent outright, and fast.

I kept digging through David's digital footprint. His name appeared on various investment sites and financial forums, usually discussing emerging technologies or pet industry trends. One post caught my eye: on a small investor message board, user "DBInvestor" was asking about patent rights and divorce proceedings.

The message was nearly identical in tone and phrasing to one of the anonymous library threats against Melissa. I checked the user's post history and found he'd made a rookie mistake. He'd once signed a post, "Best regards, David Bloom."

That connection made me wonder about the library's computer records. A few minutes with my specialized software got me into their system. The threatening posts had all been made from Computer Station 4, and the login records showed the same library card number each time: 2947.

The cardholder information was encrypted, but breaking the library's basic security took less than a minute. There it was: David Bloom. He'd gotten his card when they moved to Stewart's Crossing.

Rochester had been dozing. Now he came over and put his head on my knee. His expression was serious, like he knew we'd found another piece of the puzzle.

The timing of the posts was interesting too. Each one came right after Melissa had meetings with her patent attorney. David must have been tracking her calendar, trying to intimidate her into giving up the patent rights.

The library's security cameras would have footage of him using the computers. That would be another piece of evidence for Rick to add to his case.

I called Rick and told him what I'd learned. "David couldn't risk letting Melissa file for divorce," I said.

"Exactly. Once she filed, all marital assets would be frozen pending settlement. Including intellectual property rights."

"He'd lose everything," I said. "His investors and the people he owed money to probably wouldn't want to wait around without Melissa in the picture as an expert."

"We should sit down and go through all this," he said. "Why don't we meet at the Chocolate Ear on your way home?"

I thought about David's nervous behavior at the Chocolate Ear, his desperate phone call about accessing accounts. He wasn't just angry about Melissa's success. He was terrified of his financial house of cards collapsing.

Twenty minutes later, Rochester and I walked into the café, and Rick was already at a table in the dog-friendly section with a café mocha for me and a biscuit for Rochester. The dog took it gently and settled down on the floor to chew.

When I looked up, I saw David Bloom approaching us. "I know who killed Melissa," he said, pulling up a third chair at the table. "It was Patricia Morgan."

Rick kept his expression neutral. "How do you figure?"

"Look at this." He pulled out a stack of printed emails. "Patricia threatened Melissa about her training methods. Said she'd 'do whatever it took' to protect her business."

Rick handed them to me and I scanned them. They showed a heated professional disagreement, but nothing that suggested violence. "These are from months ago," I said.

"There's more." David leaned forward. "Patricia was working with Colin Whitaker to sabotage Melissa's collar prototypes. That's why the German Shepherd went crazy at the dog show. The two of them are in cahoots, and they wanted to discredit Melissa's work."

Rochester, lying quietly beside my chair, lifted his head and gave a soft whine.

"If Morgan and Whitaker were trying to sabotage the prototypes, why were you trying to sell similar technology to PetTech Industries last week?" Rick asked.

David's face went still. "Who told you that?"

"I'm a cop," Rick said. "I look into motives. You tried to sell Melissa's invention before she was even dead."

"Those designs were mine," he said, but his voice lacked conviction. "I funded the development. I had every right—"

"To steal her work?" I interrupted. "Or just to profit from her death?"

Rochester suddenly stood, hackles raised, staring at David's hands. Following his gaze, I noticed David's right hand had slipped into his jacket pocket.

"You don't understand," David said. His voice had changed, becoming harder. "She was going to ruin everything. Years of work, millions in potential profits, all going to waste because she wouldn't listen to reason."

"Where's Maxwell?" I asked quietly.

The question seemed to throw him. "What?"

"Your dog. The one Melissa trained. Where is he?"

David's face twisted. "At the vet. He's been... difficult since Saturday. Won't wear his collar anymore."

Rochester growled softly. Not threatening, but definitely issuing a warning. "You tested the modified collar on Maxwell first, didn't you?" I said. "That's why he's traumatized."

David's hand emerged from his pocket, empty. "You can't prove anything."

"I had Colin Whitaker analyze the collar we found in Melissa's hand the day she was murdered," Rick said. "He said it was a very early prototype, before they realized what level of stun was appropriate. He said Melissa used it in demonstrations to show what not to do."

Rick gave David a cold stare. "You waited at the park that morning. Knew she'd be there early to set up for the clinic. When she bent down to adjust the demonstration collars, you used a clicker to activate the stun feature."

David's jaw clenched. "She wouldn't listen to reason. I needed the money that we'd get from signing the patent rights over. That money would pull me out of debt, give me a chance to start over again. But she insisted that she had to retain control. Then she swore that when the divorce went through I'd get nothing, even though I was the one who supplied all her funding sources."

Rick nodded. "The stun from the collar disoriented her enough for you to get close," he continued. "I noticed you drive a Mercedes. These days they come with a telescoping lug wrench as part of their standard toolkit. It's made of chrome-plated steel and has the Mercedes logo embossed on it. It's about 19 inches long when extended."

David's mouth fell open, but he didn't say anything.

"The ME found microscopic traces of chrome plating in the wound, and the distinctive triangular shape of the impact matches the end of that kind of wrench. I'm sure that once I get a search warrant for your car, we'll find a lug wrench like that, perhaps even one with traces of Melissa's blood."

Rick continued. "And those threatening posts you made at the library? The security cameras caught you at Computer Station 4. Your visits always occurred right after Melissa met with her patent attorney." He smiled grimly. "The librarian remembered you clearly. Said you seemed agitated and kept looking over your shoulder while you typed."

"She was so small," David said quietly. "I didn't mean to hit her that hard. But she was going to ruin everything."

Rochester growled softly again. He'd known all along. The way Maxwell flinched from David's touch, the trauma response to the collar. The little Yorkie had witnessed his owner testing the modified collar on a near-deadly setting.

David's shoulders slumped. As Rick read him his rights, I looked down at Rochester, who had relaxed his alert posture.

"Good boy," I said softly.

His tail thumped once against the floor. He'd been trying to tell us about Maxwell from the beginning. The little dog's fear, his reaction to the collar, all of it pointing to David's guilt.

Rick led David quietly out through the side door, away from the handful of customers in the main café who hadn't even noticed what was happening in the dog-friendly section. But news of the arrest spread quickly through Stewart's Crossing, and it was all my dog-owning neighbors wanted to talk about when Rochester and I ran into them later on our walks.

Within days, Patricia Morgan would emerge as a key witness against David. Her testimony about his obsession with the collars, combined with evidence that he'd manipulated her professional rivalry with Melissa to create a smokescreen for his own actions, helped build the prosecutor's case. Patricia's business survived, though she quietly retired from training and sold Pawsitive Solutions to a younger trainer.

The lavender oil Rochester had sniffed at the crime scene, and at Patricia's facility, was traced to David Bloom. At Melissa's suggestion he had placed a few drops of it on Maxwell's bedding, to calm him when he was nervous. David admitted that he'd spilled some oil on his hands that morning, and that he'd grabbed Melissa's charm bracelet when they were arguing.

That summer, Colin Whitaker became an adjunct instructor in Eastern College's engineering department. With the help of students, he began refining the humane training collar design. He promised that any profits would go to a foundation in Melissa's name, supporting positive reinforcement training methods and helping shelter dogs find new homes. Her work would live on, helping the animals she had loved so much.

Soon after that, Lili showed me a photo on her phone. Maxwell was there in his new home, curled up with another Yorkie on a sunny windowsill. The local Yorkshire terrier rescue group had placed him with an experienced foster family who specialized in traumatized dogs. His tail was starting to wag again.

Sometimes the most damning evidence comes from those who can't speak, but still manage to tell the truth.

NEIL'S AUTHOR NOTES & FREE GIFT

It's a fact of life that dogs get old. To keep Rochester young and vibrant, I'm only moving the books forward a few months at a time. The first book in the series, In Dog We Trust, was published in 2010, when Rochester is a year old. That's why this story takes place in 2015.

For a free copy of "Rochester's Puppyhood," visit https://bit.ly/RochesterPup where you can download the story in your choice of formats.

In this touching prequel to the Golden Retriever Mystery series, meet Rochester before he became Steve Levitan's trusted crime-solving companion. From his challenging early days in a twelve-puppy litter to abandonment at a shelter, Rochester's journey is far from easy. But when Caroline Kelly adopts him, he finally finds the loving home he deserves—until tragedy strikes. After Caroline's murder, Rochester must help a reluctant Steve Levitan track down her killer, forging an unbreakable bond that will lead to their future adventures together. Told from Rochester's uniquely canine perspective, this heartwarming origin story reveals how a golden retriever with a nose for justice found his true calling.

If you enjoyed "Dog's Punishment," you'll want to check out the full Golden Retriever Mystery series featuring Steve Levitan and his intuitive companion Rochester. Join them as they investigate murders in and around the charming town of Stewart's Crossing, Pennsylvania, where everyone has secrets and Rochester's keen instincts often lead Steve to the truth. From *In*

Dog We Trust to *Dog Grant Me*, each book combines engaging mysteries with the special bond between a man and his dog. Steve and Rochester's adventures continue to show that sometimes the most observant detective has four legs and a tail.

And please add your review or rating wherever you get your books. Your comments help other readers find the right books for them.

Find out more at Neil's website, http://www.mahubooks.com.

LAMB CHOPPED

by Joanna Campbell Slan
Author of the Kiki Lowenstein Mystery Series

CHAPTER 1

"Let me get this straight." The police officer squinted at me, as if he was trying to decide what to believe. Scars from teenage acne pockmarked his weathered skin, and his teeth were yellow from smoking. His name badge said: Randall. The embroidered patch above his pocket showed he was part of the Webster Groves Police Department. "You've never been to this dog park before. This was your first visit. And your dog found a hand? Just a hand? No body? Sort of like Thing from the Addams Family? You wouldn't be pulling my leg, would you?"

Taking a long, slow breath through my nose, I fought to stay calm, although it felt like I was being hurled around in a blender. My stomach threatened to revolt. My eyes stung with unshed tears. My teeth were chattering. I was totally grossed out. I'd seen corpses before, but I'd never had personal contact with a disembodied body part. A mangled hand had come flying and walloped me in the chest before falling to the ground. It was too gross for words. The image of it would stick with me for a long, long time.

CHAPTER 2

Less than ten days ago, Gracie, my harlequin Great Dane, and I had arrived at Dr. Croydan's veterinary office on a promising morning in March. The weak sunlight warmed the air, and the sweet fragrance of daffodils hung over the tender sprouts of grass. Spring can alternate between glorious or treacherous in eastern Missouri. The weather swings wildly from soft breezes to violent hailstorms. Often in the course of 24 hours. All in all, my mood was upbeat, given the mild weather.

But Dr. Croydan's appearance in the examining room changed everything. He came in while looking over Gracie's chart. Instead of greeting me, the vet was shaking his head. His body language gave me a jolt of concern. Immediately, he ran his hands along Gracie's body and frowned at me.

The vet resembled a wizard from a fairytale. His face was deeply creased. Tufts of gray hair protruded from his ears, while his head was practically bald. He was angry, and his anger was directed at me. He said, "Your dog is overweight. Unless you get some of this off of her, Gracie won't make it another year."

I felt sick. Loving a big dog is an exercise in courage because their life expectancy is short. But I fell head-over-heels for Gracie when I saw her squeezed into a too-small metal crate. I didn't care that she'd cost a lot to feed, and I was struggling financially. It was love at first sight.

"Great Danes have one of the shortest life expectancies of all dogs. Their size puts stress on all their organs. Additional weight is an incredible hardship. You need to limit her access to treats and make sure she gets more exercise." Dr. Croydan glared at me.

This was all my fault. How could I have allowed Gracie to gain so much weight?

"Kiki? Mrs. Lowenstein-Detweiler? Are you listening?" Dr. Croydan sounded peeved.

"Yes," I managed. I couldn't say more because I was too choked up. Simple fact: I couldn't imagine life without Gracie. Sensing my distress, Gracie leaned her weight against me, a common Great Dane ploy for affection. Her long pink tongue landed a wet caress on my hand. I responded by massaging her behind her ears.

The doctor said, "I didn't intend to upset you. Over the years, I've found that if I'm not blunt, pet parents tend to shrug off my warnings. This extra weight needs to come off."

I stared at the floor. Hadn't I heard the same warning from my general practitioner about my own health? Yes, I had. My waistband felt tight. My blouses gaped in front. But I had ignored these signs of weight gain.

Had I personally put on extra weight? Yes, I had. So had Gracie.

Something had to be done.

I marched out of the vet's office, clutching a blue sheet from his prescription pad. Dr. Croydan's words had hit home and filled me with determination to tackle those extra pounds. The ones carried by both me and my dog.

CHAPTER 3

When we returned home, I walked into the kitchen and slumped on a chair by the table. Gracie padded over to her empty food bowl.

"How was your visit to the vet?" asked Bronwyn "Brawny" Macavity, our nanny. A Scot with military training and a degree from an elite school for childminders in the UK, Brawny keeps our household running smoothly. She even puts in a few hours at my store, teaching crochet and knitting. Over time, she's become my dear friend and confidant.

"Not good." My face flushed with embarrassment. "Gracie has gained a lot of weight. The vet was adamant about cutting back on her treats. I know the kids drop food on the floor for her, but I didn't realize she got that many extra calories. You don't give her treats, do you?"

The normally unflappable Brawny stared down at her black brogues. After a long silence, she said, "Aye, I share the odd tidbit now and again. I shall be more careful. I promise."

Later that day, when I told my husband about the vet visit, my husband Homicide Detective Chad Detweiler looked suitably chagrined. Turns out, he'd been sneaking Gracie treats, too.

The boys—Erik, age eight, and Ty, age three—were a harder sell. To them, dropping food on the floor was a natural by-product of eating. However, when I explained Gracie was too fat to be healthy, they both promised to be more careful.

Last, I told Anya, my sixteen-year-old daughter, about the vet's assertion we were killing Gracie. Not surprisingly, her eyes shone with tears. "Mom? I've been sneaking her dog yummies at night when she comes into my room. I'll stop. I promise."

In essence, everyone was indulging Gracie.

After we cleared the table from dinner that evening, I showed Brawny what the vet had written on his light-blue prescription sheet: No or low-calorie treats, in moderation. Low calorie food for mature dogs, and more exercise (preferably outside where she can romp with other dogs).

"It would seem like Gracie gets a lot of exercise here at home," I said, turning the paper over in my hand.

There were three youngsters under our roof. When you have kids, you have playdates with their friends. We had a large extended family by blood, and even more, if you included members added by choice, our "found family." That growing number of people caused a lot of commotion.

Even more chaos ensued when you added four-legged creatures into the mix. There was Monroe, the donkey, who came along with our property. He's a sweet animal, totally docile, unless you're short and dressed in a diaper. There's Seymore, my daughter Anya's pet, who had begun life as a barn cat. The gray tabby lounged his way through life. If there was a soft spot in the house, Seymore claimed it as his own. Finally, we had Martin, my ginger rescue cat, who especially loved teasing Gracie. Martin had grown from a starving ball of yellow fur into a good-sized tom with an attitude. He loved sitting on our carpeted window perches and chattering at wild birds.

Gracie took her job seriously, being the big dog in charge.

Brawny pointed out, "Chasing around after the others is not the same as consistent, regular exercise. Some days, the boys don't play with Gracie at all, and the cats are getting older. More and more they snooze in the sun."

"Hmm," I said. She was right.

Brawny stacked plates, but she didn't turn around. "Have ye thought about taking Gracie for walks?"

Yes, I had. Reluctantly.

The time had come for me to quit thinking and start walking.

CHAPTER 4

My store, Time in a Bottle, the premier crafting shop in the metro St. Louis area, is my happy place. However, at work the next morning, I was not a happy camper. I couldn't shake my concerns about Gracie's health. Nor could I ignore my solemn responsibility to help her lose that weight. I guess I wore my worries on my face. I tried to hide it from my customers, but most of them knew me too well to let it slide.

Tangela Washington was working on a set of greeting cards when she grabbed me as I walked by. Her soft hands reinforced the gentle question in her dark brown eyes. "What's wrong, Kiki? Usually, you're as bubbly as a shook-up can of cola. This morning you look like you've lost your best friend."

When I told her about the vet's warning, she nodded solemnly. "It's nearly impossible to take a walk long enough to tire my Bailey out. That's why I've been going with her to the dog park."

I admired the photo she pulled up on her phone. A liver-and-white Springer Spaniel stared up at me. On closer inspection, I could see the dog hadn't settled her weight on the floor.

Instead, she hovered, eager to spring out of the sit position. I turned my attention back to Tangela. "Wait! Didn't you used to own a Doberman?"

Her eyes filled with tears. "I did. He passed away unexpectedly."

"I'm sorry," I said. "That's hard, isn't it? Our pets are such important members of our family." I plopped down next to Tangela and set to work, rolling thin strips of paper for a quilling project. Hoping to guide us away from her grief, I said, "I'd completely forgotten there was a dog park here in Webster Groves. Remind me where it's located."

Tangela's jet-black hair was cut in a pixie style, emphasizing her strong bone structure. Her full lips lifted into a smile as she wrote an address on a scrap piece of paper. "You and your dog will love it. It's not far from here. You live nearby, right?"

"About five blocks away. Do you go to the dog park often?" I asked.

"Nearly every morning early, unless it's raining. My Bailey has so much fun! She races around until she exhausts herself. Sleeps like a baby and doesn't destroy a single sock," said Tangela with a laugh. "Before we visited regularly, Bailey ripped up at least one sock every day. She doesn't eat them, but she loves tearing them apart. She's only a pup, but she was costing me a bundle. Do you have any idea how much socks cost these days?"

"No," I said, "but if you'd like, Brawny can teach you to knit or crochet a pair. She's incredibly patient."

Raising her hands to warn me off, Tangela said, "No way am I learning another craft. Not when I already have a zillion projects started here and at home. Do not tempt me like that, Kiki. I need another hobby like I need another hole in my head. Besides. I don't trust my dog to behave herself around handmade socks! Too tempting."

We both laughed.

"Okay, seriously. You need to join me at the dog park," said Tangela, pulling up an article on her phone. I read:

Local professionals, Richard Montgomery and Dr. Ellen Blackwood, meet with other dog lovers at the Webster Groves Dog Park. The space offers a variety of amenities, including several water fountains and a spacious area for playing.

"How about tomorrow morning?" I asked, eager to solidify our new friendship. I'd always liked Tangela, but I didn't know her very well.

"It's a date. If we have time after the dogs play, we can stop by the Morning Glory Café. They have terrific coffee and fresh baked goods," Tangela said, playing with a silver necklace. A charm was attached but I didn't get a clear look at it.

"The goodies will be my treat," continued Tangela. "I used to work down the street from Morning Glory, and I am borderline addicted to their muffins."

Sounded heavenly to me.

That evening, my husband texted to say he wouldn't make dinner. Since he works homicides, this isn't unusual. But it gets tedious. He'd been handed three big cases in a row, and his busy schedule was getting old...fast. At the dinner table, our three children were fractious, a sure sign they missed their dad. I distracted them by playing a game. "Let's all share one nice thing that happened to us today," I said. "Why don't we go around the table? Anya? Can you go first?" As the oldest, she's uber-responsible.

Using the back of her hand to brush a lock of platinum hair from her eyes, she said, "We had a meeting with our college counselors today. They talked about extra-curricular activities that would help us get into the college of our choice."

"Really? Did you get any ideas?" I asked. All three of my children attend CALA, the Charles and Anne Lindbergh Academy, a very prestigious private school.

Anya made a non-committal noise. "I know I'd like to work with animals, but I'm not sure exactly what I'd want to do. Could be depressing, you know? There can be sad outcomes."

"I sure do." A lump filled my throat.

"A girl in my class helps at the pound. Her name is Jenny Sanchez. I want to talk more with her about it," said Anya.

We went next to Erik. He launched into a complicated story about the crayfish in the aquarium in his homeroom. I did my best to follow, although the narrative was confusing. The upshot was that Erik really, really liked the crayfish, and he would have really, really liked to bring one home except he figured one of our cats might gobble it down as a snack.

"Sad to say, I think you're right, buddy. The cats won't understand the crayfish is a new pet. Sorry about that. Brawny, you're next." I gave her a nod.

She was learning intarsia crochet, which offers a tidy way to switch colors several times while creating fabric. She excused herself and came back with a lovely piece in a rainbow of shades. I couldn't wait for her to teach me what she'd learned.

Ty, the youngest, had been sitting and listening politely. "What do you have to share, Ty?" I asked with a big smile, knowing how mischievous he could be. We'd put him in school early because the child is super-smart and high energy. Keeping him occupied is a challenge. He sat up straighter in his chair and said, "I drew dinosaurs." With that, he hopped down and came back with three sheets of crayon-colored representations that were, indeed, dinosaurs. Actually, his renderings were impressive for someone so young.

"What about you, Mom?" Anya cocked her head."

"One of my customers told me about a dog park within

walking distance. Gracie and I both could use the exercise and fresh air. I'm going over early tomorrow," I said.

While the rest of us went back to admiring Ty's artwork, Anya looked up the dog park on her phone. (Yes, she was breaking the rule of no phones at the table, but I let it slide this time.)

"Good reviews on Yelp," she said. "Seems like the owners who go there are responsible pet parents. All the dogs are supposed to have their shots. Any pooch who misbehaves is banned. Looks like a cool place to take Gracie."

My husband got home late that night and was gone early the next day, leaving me with the memory of a quick peck on the cheek and a whispered, "I love you, babe. Have a good day."

I didn't get the chance to tell him I was going to the dog park that morning. He would hear about my plans later when I phoned him in a panic.

CHAPTER 5

No one in the house was awake when I clipped the leash on Gracie, slipped into a sweater I'd crocheted, and headed out. It was an easy walk. The closer we got to the park, the more alert my dog became, sniffing the air and lifting her uncropped ears as she availed herself of all her senses.

A discreet sign hanging on the cyclone fencing announced we'd arrived at the Webster Groves Community Dog Park. The park itself was divided into areas for small dogs (under 22 pounds) and larger ones. A double-gated system of entry prevented runaways. The landscape was a mix of young grass, slowly peeping through the spring-warmed dirt, and patches of gravel surrounding fountains designed to make drinking easy for canine visitors. Fake fire hydrants dotted other gravel patches scattered across the landscape. Near the gates sat a row of park benches, presumably for pet parents to occupy while they watched the fun. A low hedge of spirea ran around the margins, buffering the park from those few houses with yards nearby. Slowly, this entire neighborhood was moving from residential to retail. Such was the evolution of communities. Either they died or they grew, and if their fate involved the latter, they inevitably gobbled up property.

Right now, Gracie and I had the place all to ourselves. I'd overestimated the time it would take us to walk from the house, so we'd gotten there early. Since Tangela hadn't arrived yet, I paused outside the gates and read the posted rules, which began with a warning:

You assume all risks for yourself and your pet when you enter the park.

1. Clean up after your dog: Pick up your dog's waste and dispose of it properly. We try to keep bags available, but it's always a good idea to bring your own.

2. Leash your dog: Keep your dog on a leash until you're inside the appropriate fenced-in area of the park. A leash is always a good idea in case your pet becomes overly excited.

3. Leave aggressive dogs at home: Aggressive dogs are not allowed in any dog park.

4. Bring no toys except tennis balls: Toys can cause even mild-mannered dogs to quarrel.

5. Monitor your dog: Keep an eye on your dog at all times. Your pet is your responsibility.

6. Vaccinations must be up-to-date: Make sure your dog is current on their vaccinations, especially those for contagious illnesses. This includes a rabies shot.

7. Don't leave gates open: Don't leave the dog park gates open at any time.

8. Avoid humping.

I couldn't help but laugh at that last request. Patting Gracie, I said, "I'm assuming they mean the dogs should avoid humping.

Or are they talking about the pet parents? Is this a filming venue for episodes of Only Fans? Hmm? Let's find out.

The first gate clanked shut behind us. A few steps later and we went through the second gate, allowing us admittance to the big dog arena.

Taking a moment to get my bearings, I chose a nearby park bench and plopped down. Gracie trembled with eagerness. Her muscles strained with anticipation. Her tail was high and alert as she sniffed the air with great concentration. That wasn't surprising. She was picking up pee-mail, a tantalizing tsunami of olfactory messages.

"Kiki!"

I turned to see Tangela struggling with a liver-and-white Springer Spaniel that bounced up and down like a child's pogo stick. After waving hello, I unclipped Gracie's leash. Now that Tangela had arrived, I was sure we'd be sticking around.

Gracie took off across the grass like a spitball out of a peashooter. The Springer Spaniel yodeled sadly, crying after Gracie, and making it obvious she hated being left behind.

But Tangela didn't unleash Bailey. Not immediately. Instead, she fumbled with removing a navy raincoat. She was also trying to keep a grip on a tote bag and a cardboard drink carrier. Her efforts were complicated because a very excited Bailey kept twisting her leash around Tangela's legs.

"Let me help," I said, offering to take Tangela's bag.

"I got us coffee on the way here," explained a breathless Tangela. "My second cup of the day. Figured we might as well enjoy a hot drink while the pups had their fun. Where did Gracie go?"

I scanned the park and was rewarded with a glimpse of black-and-white fur, half burrowed in a row of shrubbery in the far-right corner. Gracie's long tail waved like a flag run up a pole. Obviously, she was having fun. "Back in those shrubs," I said, chinning over my shoulder and setting Tangela's bag on the park bench.

Bailey strained at her leash, her anxious gaze going from Tangela to Gracie.

"Bailey, you are not getting another treat," said Tangela, wagging an index finger at her baby.

To me, Tangela said, "Bailey can be such a chow hound. A real beggar when food's involved. You seem like a 'two sugars and two creams' type of woman. Am I right?"

"Absolutely." The proffered paper cup had a brown corrugated wrapper stamped with a bright blue flower. I was blowing on the liquid when, out of the corner of my eye, I glimpsed dirt flying in the air. Gracie was in full dirt-digging mode. I cupped my free hand around my mouth and yelled, "Gracie? What are you doing? Stop it!"

But she didn't listen. I grumbled to myself. The coffee was delicious. I wanted to savor it, and I didn't want to chase after my pup. But if I didn't, Gracie would soon be a filthy mess. Fortunately, Tangela had not unclipped her dog or we would have had two dirty dogs.

Soil kept flying all around Gracie like she was a ditch digger gone crazy. There was no recourse for me other than to bring her back and calm her down. Putting my paper cup on the bench, I said to Tangela, "Hang on."

I sprinted across the yard. "Gracie? Stop it!"

She raised that blocky head to acknowledge me and immediately resumed digging. Even from a distance, I could see her legs were covered with fresh dirt. She went back to her urgent task, only moving faster, because she knew the moment I reached her I would try to drag her away.

I was ten feet from my dog when a human hand slammed into my chest and fell to the ground.

A hand.

Severed.

Unattached.

Tossed up by Gracie's digging.

But it couldn't be real. Could it? I squatted for a better look.

Oh, yeah. It was real.

CHAPTER 6

With trembling fingers, I dialed 911. After telling the dispatcher my location and the fact I'd found a stray body part, I disconnected the call. I hit speed-dial and phoned my husband. He listened while I struggled to make a coherent plea. "Can you come? I'm not hurt, but I am upset."

"Stay where you are and keep the dogs away from the body part," he said.

Dragging Gracie by the collar, I returned to the bench.

"What's wrong?" Tangela asked. Her face was tense with concern as she shifted her weight from one foot to the other. Her cup and mine were both gone. Presumably, she'd tossed them in the metal trash container soldered to the fence.

"Gracie dug up a body part." I could scarcely believe what I was reporting.

"A what?" Tangela's voice climbed higher than the lazy clouds overhead.

"Didn't you see that thing? Flying through the air? The unidentified object that smacked me in the chest? I got a good look at it. I'm pretty sure it's a severed hand."

"A h-h-h-hand? Just a hand? No body?" Tangela turned pale.

"Just a hand. You might want to put your head between your knees rather than faint. I've already dialed 911. I could be wrong about what that thing is. It was pretty mangled. But they'll send people…and those people will sort this out." In a soft voice, I continued, "I also called my husband. He's a cop. You probably already know that."

Tangela shook her head. "Lord above. How on earth did this happen? How could everything go so wrong?"

I could have said, Easy-peasy. We were the first people at the park. My dog sniffed out a tantalizing smell. She followed it and dug up a body part. See? That's exactly how this happened.

But honestly, I did not want to go over the sequence of events. What I wanted was to drop my face into my hands and pretend none of this was happening. I had gotten up this morning expecting a fun, relaxed outing with my dog. A bit of much needed exercise. A chance to get to know Tangela better.

That's not what I'd gotten. Now Tangela and I sat stoically, side by side, and waited for a Webster Groves police car to pull up.

When it did, out popped a strange little man in a blue and black uniform. Ironically, he was shaped exactly like one of the toy fireplugs that dotted the dog park. His complexion was a florid red, and his skin bore the scars of teenage acne. His hair was thinning, and its color was indeterminate. I work with color all day long, but I couldn't have put a name to it.

Hoisting his Sam Browne belt, the uniformed cop came toward us, moving with a strange gait caused by a pair of bow legs. They would have fit perfectly on a cow poke. On a small-town cop, they bordered on ridiculous.

As he came closer, I read his name badge: Randall. But Randall did not come alone. He brought with him an attitude. He stared at us. Glowering at me, at Tangela, and our dogs.

Rather than check to see if we were okay, he heaved a supercilious sniff. "One of you phoned 911? What seems to be the problem here, ladies?"

Mentally, I'd rehearsed what I wanted to say. A cogent narrative. Despite my best efforts, my words came out slightly jumbled. "My dog...Gracie...digging...dirt going every which way...walked over to stop her...hit by a flying hand...got nasty stuff all over my best handmade sweater."

"Uh-huh." Officer Randall looked distinctly unimpressed. "You got a name, lady?"

I introduced myself and waited while Tangela did the same.

"A hand, you say? You sure you didn't get the wrong end of a prank? One of them plastic gloves people fill up with candy for Halloween?"

"I'm certain that what hit me is real. You can go see for yourself."

He did, and when he came back, his rosy cheeks had turned white.

After that, he yammered on and on. Something about other officers joining us, even though the department was shorthanded. He complained about his duty as the first responder to secure the scene. He wandered back to his car, grabbed a bunch of wood stakes, and began sticking them randomly in the ground. Tangela and I sat there like two lumps of dough.

One by one, more patrol cars pulled up. As law enforcement authorities swarmed around us, I stared at them but couldn't interpret what I saw. Shock. Everyone reacts to it differently. As my body struggled with the urge for fight or flight, I lost track of what was happening.

"Kiki!" A familiar voice cut through the crackle of the radios and conversations of first responders. I jumped to my feet and ran, nearly tripping over Gracie, as she was determined to beat me to her main squeeze, my husband Homicide Detective Chad

Detweiler. Throwing myself into his arms brought a huge sense of relief. He whispered in my ear, "You okay? I came as fast as I could."

"Yes," I said quietly. "A little rattled, but otherwise, okay."

Behind us, Officer Randall cleared his throat. I didn't care. He could clear his throat until the cows came home. I was not about to turn loose of my husband. In fact, I stayed stuck to him like a strip of Velcro, doing a partial backbend as Detweiler reached out to offer Officer Randall a handshake. "Detective Chad Detweiler with the St. Louis County Police."

Officer Randall gave a petulant little snort. "I've heard about you. Big shot with the Major Case Squad, right? You live here locally? Yeah, I guessed as much." The cop's voice was more snarky than friendly.

"That's right," said Detweiler, ignoring Officer Randall's attempts to get under his skin. "We live in the old Haversham house. My wife Kiki has a business a few blocks away. I see you've met her? So help me get up to speed. What exactly do we have here?"

Even with my face pressed against my husband's jacket, I knew Officer Randall was wavering. Detweiler's superior experience had trumped him, and he was smart enough to know it. But would he back down? Or would he insist on acting like the big man? My husband had no jurisdiction here. I'd phoned Detweiler right after I dialed 911, the way any other wife would call her spouse in an upsetting situation. After all, it wasn't every day I got hit in the chest by a disembodied hand. A gross, bloody hand complete with shredded tendrils of sinew and flesh.

Just when I'd decided this situation couldn't get worse... it did

A yell came from a crime scene investigator who'd been poking around in the shrubs near where Gracie had discovered the hand. A second CSI tech hurried over to help. Soon, there was a lot more shouting. Officer Randall excused himself, saying, "We're short one detective, so I'm in charge. You stay put."

My husband and I did exactly that. Gracie yawned and lay down at our feet. She rested her head on her front paws in a deceptively lady-like way.

"What do you suppose is going on?" I asked, after glancing toward the cluster of professionals.

"Not sure. If Officer Randall is in charge of securing the scene, he isn't doing a good job. The yellow tape isn't in place. I don't see anybody monitoring who's coming and going." Detweiler made a little huffing sound. "Best guess? They found another body part."

Actually, he was wrong.

They'd discovered a nearly intact corpse.

CHAPTER 7

Time seemed to drag on and on. I was leaning against my husband when Officer Randall finally came back, shaking his head. "At least we know where that hand came from," he muttered.

"Pardon?" my husband asked.

"That dog of yours discovered more than a stray hand. A body is back there, too, behind the spirea bushes. I'm pretty certain that's where the hand came from." Officer Randall looked green around the gills, as my grandmother used to say. It's hard to play the part of a tough guy when you're struggling not to puke.

An ambulance pulled up and uniformed medics climbed out. They weren't in a hurry because there was no need to rush. As we watched, they unloaded a wheeled gurney and a black body bag.

"It's going to take them a while," said Detweiler, almost to himself. "They'll need to take pictures, search the area, and whatnot."

"Well, now," said Officer Randall, drawing out each word. Although he sounded authoritative, his voice had definitely climbed a notch. "Since we're short on staff, I've been authorized to take your wife's statement. I don't suppose it would hurt none for you to listen in. As a courtesy. Seeing as how you don't have jurisdiction here."

Yes, Officer Randall had to drive home his point. He was the local constabulary, as they say in British crime fiction. My husband was the outsider. So, the Webster Groves cop was angling for a nod to his status. He wanted us to stroke his ego, and he wasn't about to give up his sliver of importance easily. I wasn't surprised. Not really.

The St. Louis metro area has 91 different municipalities. They don't all play nicely with each other. Fortunately, Detweiler has gotten very good at bobbing, weaving, and making nice with the other law enforcement agencies. Rather than get all humpy about Officer Randall's snooty manner, my husband nodded and said, "Thank you, Officer. Much obliged. We're on your turf. If you're ready to take Kiki's statement, lead the way."

And so, my first visit to the Webster Groves Dog Park was also my last. At least for a long, long time.

I'd planned a fun outing with Gracie, giving her much needed exercise while I visited with Tangela and her pup, Bailey. Instead, I found myself embroiled in a murder investigation.

Correction: Another murder investigation.

See, we all have special talents. Things we do really well. And we also have proclivities. For example, there are folks who get hit by lightning, over and over. Folks who have fender-benders almost monthly. Me? I get involved in murder investigations. Not by choice. Not by design. By some cosmic fluke I can't explain.

Murders happen. When they do, they often spill over into my life. I am that innocent bystander who gets sucked in. Over the years, I've learned to handle this quirk with less drama. I was at the beach one day when I had an epiphany: Life is like dealing with the ocean. If you get caught in the undertow, don't fight it. You'll only exhaust yourself. Instead, let the rip current carry you along. Eventually, it will spit you out. As my husband and I followed the sidewalk to the community center, I did my best to accept my fate. This was not the lovely morning I'd planned for.

I'd made this doggy play date, hoping for a healthy change of pace.

Instead, I'd stepped into an ugly mess. And it had all begun so innocently.

CHAPTER 8

Once inside the Community Center, Officer Randall asked us to wait while he secured a conference room. I was too keyed up to sit still. While my husband returned phone calls for work, I wandered the halls.

The various wall-mounted display cabinets captured my attention. Several blue ribbons were tacked to one corkboard. In the center was a photo of a patrician-looking woman holding a large blue ribbon in one hand while her other hand pulled on the collar of a gorgeous Rottweiler. A caption explained that MaryBeth Montgomery, a local woman, was the proud owner of an AKC Grand Champion.

The next display case bore the headline: "Community Center Fishing Trip." Catfish noodling, or catching catfish by sticking your hand in their holes, is illegal here in Missouri, but it's a booming sport across the river in Illinois. These photos showed various men and one woman holding up big honking fishes. In a larger group picture, the participants received awards, although the woman didn't look happy about it. Catfish look like aliens, thanks to their long, snake-like whiskers. No way would I encourage them to mistake my fingers for bait.

Officer Randall led us to a room with a computer. My husband listened silently as I gave the officer my statement. Detweiler was dialing it back, so the Webster Groves cop didn't feel disrespected.

Afterward, Detweiler took Gracie and me home. Tangela had already left with Bailey. That made sense because she had less to say. After all, she was merely a bystander, not the person who'd had a close encounter with a stray body part.

"This is a first," my husband said, shaking his head. "Maybe we should enroll Gracie in cadaver dog school. I bet she'd sail through her courses with flying colors."

"Or flying body parts," I said as I stared out the window of his cruiser. "I've never been hit by a dismembered hand before. This is a new low. Or high. Or whatever."

A crime scene investigator had relieved me of my crocheted granny square sweater in order to check it for evidence. That made me grumpy. I'd worked hard to make that garment, and I'd been proud of it. I knew I'd get it back, but when?

"I wonder how Tangela is. I should probably call her." I picked at a spot of dirt on my jeans. I hadn't even had the chance to enjoy my coffee. Now I was stuck with a growling tummy and a growing headache from lack of caffeine.

Detweiler didn't take his eyes off the road, and his voice was flat. "I'm not sure that's a good idea. After all, both of you are suspects."

"That's ridiculous!" I said. "She was there with me when I found the hand."

Detweiler said nothing. Usually, I can guess at what he's thinking. This morning, not so much. Eager to change the subject, I said, "I suppose this means the dog park is closed." I reached over and scratched Gracie's ear. She was resting her head on Detweiler's shoulder as he drove.

"For a while, at least. Why? Are you eager to go back to the scene of the crime? Who knows what Gracie might dig up this time?"

"Yeah," I said, with a hint of amusement in my voice. "Who knows? Actually, I need to go back to the house and change. I'm scheduled for work."

After Detweiler dropped us off, I stripped down and dragged Gracie into the laundry room shower. I didn't want her depositing dirt all over the house. Since Brawny was dropping the kiddos off at school, I had the house to myself. That was good, because Gracie has been known to bolt from the shower and race madly through the house with me in naked pursuit. To her, the chase is great fun. To me, it's a hassle I could do without. This time, we got through the whole ordeal of getting clean without a hitch. I even had the chance to dry Gracie a little with my hair dryer.

After that, I threw on a pair of old jeans and a Time in the Bottle tee shirt, and made myself a toasted slice of Dave's Killer Cinnamon Raisin Bread with a thick slathering of Kerry Gold butter. Next, I fixed myself a travel mug of coffee before staring long and hard at Gracie. "You've already had a busy day, haven't you? Feel up to going into the store?"

The lift of her uncropped ears told me she was good to go… and so we went.

CHAPTER 9

Gracie's spirits seemed dampened as she waited beside me while I unlocked the back door of Time in a Bottle. My shop. My own business. My own little world. Our colorful displays of craft papers, the showcased projects, and the variety of supplies, always put me in a good mood. But even those positive triggers couldn't completely blot out what I'd seen that morning at the dog park.

I switched on the lights and sighed deeply. At Time in a Bottle, we not only save memories, we create new ones that crowd out old and ugly experiences. I love what I do.

Unleashing Gracie, I bustled about, filling her water bowl and shaking out her dog bed.

"What's up with you?" asked Clancy, my right-hand person and all-around best pal when she walked in through the back. She's a classic and somewhat imperious-looking woman who could easily pass as Jackie Kennedy's twin sister. She knows me so well that it had only taken one look for her to realize I was off-kilter.

As fast as possible, I sketched out my morning. The best part of my recitation was watching her expression change from curious to skeptical and finally pausing on horrified. Clancy moaned. "You need to be locked up. Disaster flows in your wake."

"No, it doesn't. Kiki is a catalyst for good and bad." A piping voice came from the back of the store. My other full-timer—teasingly called my "left-hand" person—had arrived. Nona Perkins reminded everyone of a plump wren. That is, of course, if wrens came equipped with psychic powers. Her special talents can make Nona annoying, if you're the type of person who hates being one-upped. And I am. But I'm learning to put aside my competitive nature and appreciate her unique insights. So what if she's a know-it-all? She is, most of the time, right about stuff. I keep telling myself to relax and trust her more.

This morning, she embraced me in a patchouli drenched hug and rocked me like I was a baby. The gesture was weirdly comforting and a little much for my tastes. I pulled away.

"Nearby negative forces have been circling each other for months," said Nona, after accepting my need for space. "They operated on different planes of existence, but Kiki moves between planes, and thus, she inadvertently connected the dots. That's all."

Looking back over her shoulder while she started the electric kettle in preparation to make tea, she asked, "Are you all right, Kiki dear? You were hit, metaphorically and physically, rather hard. By the way, you will get your sweater back. Don't fret about it."

As usual, Nona's casual shift from reality to "woo-woo/out-there" happened in the blink of an eye. Rather dizzying, actually. But I do my best to keep up.

I accepted the cup of Earl Grey tea and thanked her. Clancy glared at our friend

"Good one, Nona," she snarled. "Kiki has a horrible experience, and you brush it off like it was—"

"A clod of dirt stuck onto the sole of her shoe," supplied Nona, looking pleased with herself. Before she could say more, there came a knocking at our front door. I'd completely forgotten to unlock it, and the clock on the wall said we should have opened five minutes ago.

Thus, our workday began.

CHAPTER 10

Try as I might, I couldn't get the image of the disconnected hand out of my mind. During the workday, I kept losing my train of thought as I talked with customers. Eventually, I took a quick break. I tucked myself into a quiet corner of the sales floor and phoned Tangela, hoping a debrief over our shared trauma would help me put the crisis behind me.

"Yes?" she answered the phone curtly. That tone of voice threw me off.

"Are you okay?" I asked. What I really meant to say was, "I'm feeling miserable. You, too?"

"Of course," she said. "I love being interrogated by cops, don't you? But then, you had your hubby by your side. Must have been nice."

I stared at the phone like it had bitten me. This was not what I'd imagined Tangela would say. Before I could assemble the correct response, a customer tapped me on the shoulder. A quick look around explained that all my employees were busy helping other people. Yet another reminder we needed more worker bees.

I blurted into my phone, "Okay, Tangela. I've got to run."

As I helped my customer find the exact right shade of glitter, I reviewed that horrible scene at the dog park. My emotions were jumbled. Yet somehow, I felt guilty. Like I'd ruined Tangela's morning, too.

But why? I had done nothing wrong. She'd been the one who brought up the dog park and invited me to meet her there. It wasn't my fault my dog had found a gruesome surprise.

I ducked into the bathroom and splashed my face with cold water. The chilling temperature functioned like a gentle slap, changing my mood. Patting myself dry, I tried to put Tangela out of my mind.

At five, we locked the front door, and my crew went home. The store was closed to walk-in customers. I had a thirty-minute break before I'd re-open to a handful of crafters with reservations. This would be a special "Craft & Chat" session that I host every Thursday evening.

Tonight I would teach them how to turn coffee filters into paper daffodils. The project was simple but elegant. We would color the paper filters with water-soluble markers, let them dry, and cut them into floral silhouettes. Then we'd glue them onto cards. I greeted my students, and we got started.

We were well into our crafting session when Mabel Henderson said, "Kiki? I heard you were at the dog park this morning when they found Archie Wellington's body." Her scissors paused mid-stroke as she trimmed a blossom. Mabel was in her early fifties. Her sleek blonde bob was heavily sprayed into place, and tiny pearl earrings framed her face.

"Archie who?" I repeated.

"Archie Wellington," said Mabel.

That was the victim's name? Had he really been identified that quickly? I didn't know what to say. Identifications can be wrong. It happens.

"Yes, the dead man was definitely Archie Wellington. Local developer. Patron of the arts. Snappy dresser. Never seen without his gold signet ring. They say it was on his hand, even though the hand was not attached to his body. And you found him. Or at least, your dog found a part of him. Aren't you going to tell us about it, Kiki?" Mabel stared at me, daring me to talk. She's usually mild-mannered, but I could tell she wouldn't back down about this.

How had she gotten the news so fast? I couldn't guess.

"How'd you hear I was there at the dog park?" I asked with raised eyebrows. In the cartoon-like voice of a gangster, I turned my pencil into a fake cigar and squinted at Mabel. "Who ratted me out? I've got a bone to pick with them."

Of course, my gangster imitation caused laughter

Mabel was not about to drop the subject. She kept talking. "I know you were at the dog park, Kiki, because my mother lives in the apartment complex for folks older than 55. It's kitty-corner from the park. She's heard me talk about you and seen photos of your dog. She actually took an elevator to the sixth-floor activity room and brought along her binoculars so she could stare down into the park. That's how she recognized you and your Great Dane."

The other two women laughed softly at the mention of Mabel's mother. One of them murmured, "Nosy parker."

"Busted," I said. "Yes, I was there with Gracie. Yes, she dug something up." I gave an elaborate shrug and concluded, "But I have no idea who the victim was. None."

"Oh, I can tell you that with certainty," continued Mabel. "I have my resources. It was definitely Archie Wellington. For sure."

Mabel's friend, Lulu Chen, spoke up. "I heard it was Archie, too. Word spread like wildfire when the medics brought in the body bag. No one is sorry that man is dead. Not even the tax collector." Lulu slammed down her bottle of Aleene's Tacky Glue. The reaction was purely for emphasis, and she definitely made her point.

Mabel prodded. "What happened, Kiki? Dish!"

All eyes turned from her to me and back once more, as if we were in a tennis match. I said, "It's true. I was there. Gracie found a body part."

Hearing her name, my dog came over and sat beside me. Hoping to change the subject, I asked, "So...you didn't much care for Mr. Wellington?"

Lulu cursed under her breath. Yet another surprise in a day full of them. She's always struck me as a very proper type of person, but she was definitely adept at using adult language. She said, "What a wretched excuse for a human being Archie Wellington is. Was. That man was on a never-ending crusade against all animals, saying they were dirty, filthy, vicious creatures. He didn't much like animal owners, either. Wellington wasn't even an equal opportunity hater. He hated some breeds more than others. Big dogs in particular."

Mabel warmed to her topic. "Did you know he proposed a $500 fine for any dog caught doing its business on Webster Groves' sidewalks? Even if it was a first offense?"

"Called it a 'public menace,'" said Theresa Sanchez, chiming in. "Didn't matter if the owner cleaned up the mess immediately, he wanted the pet owner to be fined. And that was only the beginning."

Lulu's dark auburn bob framed her pretty face as she said, "Archie Wellington tried several times to shut down the dog park. At first, he complained about the noise. His house is right around the corner from the park. And yes, occasionally the dogs do bark. You know which place is his. It's that big Victorian? In shades of red, white, and blue? Then he presented the council with a fancy impact study claiming dog parks decrease local property values. Finally, he brought in a lawyer and threatened to sue the city. He says—said—the dog park is an unwarranted municipal burden on taxpayers, a noise hazard, and an unfair use of taxpayer funds."

"Wow," I said, because I didn't know what else to say. Sounded to me to like Archie Wellington had a long list of gripes.

Leaning in and speaking quietly, Theresa Sanchez looked around furtively, although the store was empty except for us. "Actually, I heard he had wanted to turn the dog park into a parking lot. He was big into redevelopment projects. Shops. Apartment buildings. To make his vision work, the city would definitely need more parking."

"But do we want more parking?" asked Lulu. "I moved here because I wanted to live in a sleepy little town. If I'd wanted to live in a place with more traffic, I'd have chosen somewhere else."

CHAPTER 11

The women were on a roll.

"Don't forget Archie Wellington's also the one who behind that awful mandatory neutering program. He got the city council to approve it, although I don't know how," Theresa said as her scissors snipped at a coffee filter with extra vigor, turning a daffodil into a chrysanthemum.

She said, "My daughter, Jenny, works at the pound as a volunteer, and she is really upset about that change. The new law states any animal brought into the shelter has to be surgically neutered within 24 hours. No grace period, no trying to find the owners first. Doesn't matter if it's a weekend or holiday. Nothing matters but—" and for emphasis she held the scissors high and went snip-snip

"What a lot of fuss and bother," Lulu chimed in. "A neighbor of ours, Richard Montgomery, is vehemently opposed to that law. He spoke eloquently at the city council meeting. Richard is the guy who runs that fancy dog breeding service? Um, he raises Rottweilers?"

"No, he doesn't run a dog breeding service," interrupted Theresa. "His wife is the one who breeds Rottweilers."

"Aren't they divorced?" asked Mabel.

Lulu put a finger to her lips and thought this over. "I believe you're right."

Theresa gave a self-satisfied nod. "The split happened recently. Richard is a good egg, but kind of a dim bulb, if you get my drift."

Actually, her mixed metaphors had me confused. Was the man a "dim bulb" or a "good egg" or a combination of both? I remembered reading his name in the article Tangela showed me about the dog park.

"Okay, right," grumbled Lulu. "A lot of people spoke up against Archie Wellington's proposal for immediate neutering. One person said you can't just take a scalpel to someone's property without their permission. And to do it so fast? A woman in the audience asked, What if your dog slips out without you noticing? What if you're out of town? What if you don't know your pet is missing? An attorney suggested the city could incur legal problems by moving so fast. Neutering an animal that quickly could be perceived as willful destruction of property."

Mabel nodded. "But Wellington laughed at all of them. He said owners should be neutered along with their animals. He came right out and said that he hated all animals. Said they are dirty and disgusting."

Theresa's hands trembled as she dropped her scissors onto the table with a clatter. "That's not the worst of what he was up to," she said, lowering her voice. "Since Jenny has been working at the pound, she's noticed their euthanasia numbers weren't adding up. Too many animals were marked as 'disposed of,' but there were no remains. Jenny started documenting everything. Times, dates, descriptions, and which animals disappeared. Last week, she did a stake-out. She followed a van that left the pound at midnight. It went to a research facility down in Joplin."

My stomach tied itself into a knot. Given Anya's interest in animal rights and the fact she knew Jenny from school, my daughter might have gone along for the ride! Yes, checking out the van's movements was a smart idea, but it had also been a very dangerous stunt. What if Anya had accompanied Jenny? What if the creeps selling dogs had spotted them? Those goons would not have let two young women interfere with their plans to make a lot of money.

There followed a tiny sniffle as Mabel fought back a sob. I was surprised because she never struck me as an emotional type of person. I shoved a box of tissues her way.

Mabel dabbed her eyes and continued, "We can guess where those poor animals went. You do know that Missouri has the largest dog auctions in the United States? Well, we do. What's more, Missouri has the largest number of commercial dog breeders with problematic inspection reports, according to the Humane Society of the United States. This state is cruel to our animal friends."

A lump of emotion filled my throat, and I wished I hadn't heard this. I had no doubt Mabel was accurate. I'd read stories that backed her up. But today of all days, I didn't want to hear it.

The whole table went silent.

There were times when I wished my customers did not feel quite so comfortable sharing with each other. Topics like sending animals to a research facility were trigger points, bound to upset almost everybody. How could Time in a Bottle be a happy place under the weight of such grim conversations?

Well, we were knee-deep in it now. Nothing to do but try to steer the Titanic away from the looming iceberg.

"What happened to Jenny's notes? She still has them, doesn't she?" I asked Theresa. Going back to facts is always helpful when emotions run high.

"Jenny took her evidence to her supervisor," Theresa said. "Next day, Wellington showed up at the pound. Gosh, but he was steamed. He told my daughter that he had influence on the shelter's board of directors. If she hoped to continue as a volunteer, she should focus on shoveling dog poop and leave thinking to smarter people. Jenny was upset, of course. Later, her boss assured her that hiring and firing of volunteers was her decision. Wellington had simply been spouting off. Even so, my child was really shaken up. Fortunately, she has a good head on her shoulders. That said, I am worried. We've since taken precautions."

"Meaning what?" asked Mabel.

"Among other things, we've safeguarded the information," said Theresa, raising her chin in defiance. "Jenny scanned every document onto a memory stick. We duplicated it onto a second stick, and I've locked a copy away."

Theresa trailed off and glanced around as if frightened. "Maybe I've said too much," she finished lamely. "I am worried about Jenny's safety. Especially given what happened today in the dog park. Sure, Archie Wellington was a miserable excuse for a man, but murder? That's appalling. Also, it happened too close to home. That information Jenny surfaced? It has to be part of a bigger deal. Someone is buying those strays. Where there's money, there's motivation for mischief."

"Nobody is here but the three of us," I hastened to reassure her.

"Four of us," said Theresa, correcting me. We all laughed, and that broke the tension. They know I'm abysmal with numbers.

"I don't count because I can't count," I said with a laugh

But Theresa still looked spooked. It can happen that way. One minute you're talking and the next you realize you might have said too much. The other women stared at the worktable with unsettled expressions. This was not the sort of happy get-together we usually enjoyed. Mabel blew her nose and said in a high-handed way, "I'm surprised you let Jenny continue working at the shelter under those circumstances, Theresa."

That was cruel and unnecessary, and it hacked Theresa off. She gathered herself to her full height and glared at Mabel. "My husband and I did our best to convince Jenny to quit on the spot, but she's committed. In fact, this volunteer experience has set her course for life. She wants to be an attorney and specialize in animal rights. Originally, she'd taken the job at the pound to boost her community involvement resume for her college applications. But you are right about one thing, Mabel. There is nothing on this green earth worth putting my child in danger. I really wish she would quit her work at the shelter. I am worried her job is dangerous. All the proof I need is that dead body in the dog park. And Kiki found that for me."

CHAPTER 12

As if finding a severed hand hadn't been enough to rock my world, Archie Wellington's threats to Jenny had made me even more jumpy. What sort of grown man tries to scare a teen like that? Obviously, someone who was ruthless. Was it possible his death was in retaliation for similar behavior? Was the attack on him only the beginning in a feud between pet owners and everyone else? I was glad for the ladies to walk me to my car. Gladder still that I had Gracie as my co-pilot. She sat prim and ladylike in the passenger's seat, her square head watching the world go by. No one with any sense would have approached my car.

I exhaled once we got home, and the garage door rolled shut. I hadn't realized I was holding my breath during the drive, but I must have done. At times like this, I appreciated my dog's presence as a deterrent.

Detweiler wasn't back from work. The house was quiet, so I went straight upstairs, climbed into bed, and fell asleep almost immediately.

The next morning, I could tell by the ruffled covers that my husband had, indeed, joined me during the night. I'd slept through his appearance. Throwing on clothes and washing my face, I hurried downstairs and into the kitchen. It was early enough that all the kids were still asleep.

"How long have you been up?" I asked, giving Detweiler a peck on the cheek. Turned out, he'd been downstairs for a good hour

"I heard you rustling around and started a second pot of coffee," he said. "I drank the first one while going through my emails. Let me get you up to speed. I was named to the Major Case Squad, so I caught the dog park case. We've had confirmation of identity. The dead man was Archie Wellington."

That dovetailed with what I'd heard the night before. I said nothing, only listened.

"I have a beef with Officer Randall. He was supposed to make sure the scene was secure, and he didn't. Too sloppy by half. We found a few things, and I'm worried there's more. When they moved the body, forensics found a crushed paper coffee cup from the Morning Glory Café. The surveillance footage from the restaurant came in this morning. Mr. Wellington definitely showed up. We've been told our victim stopped there every day at the same time for a vanilla latte before walking to work. The café opens at six.

"The CCTV shows a figure in a dark coat, standing close to Mr. Wellington. While the barista's back was turned, the mystery person sprinkled powder into Mr. Wellington's drink. The dosing was smooth. Practiced almost. Mr. Wellington never even noticed."

"Any idea who did it?" I asked, my voice breaking.

"No. Could be a man or a woman. The person was smart. He shielded his face with a hood."

Detweiler took a sip of his coffee. "Here's the thing. Someone knew exactly when Mr. Wellington would be there and what drink he'd order. The white powder didn't show up against the vanilla foam. The killer had must have studied Mr. Wellington's routine."

He consulted his notes and said, "Lab results came back on Mr. Wellington's stomach contents. Traces of Ambien were there, along with coffee. He'd had enough of the drug to make him unsteady on his feet but not enough to end his life."

"So the killer wanted Wellington impaired but conscious." I shivered, imagining Archie Wellington stumbling into the dog park, fighting to stay awake while his killer...did what? Egged him on? Led him by the arm? Held him at gunpoint?

"Here's an important question: Why there? Why in the dog park?" Detweiler asked, but I had a feeling he was talking more to himself than to me.

I reached over and squeezed his hand. "It takes effort to get inside the park. You'd have to be functional to open the latches and pass through the staggered gates."

"Good point," he said. "I'll make sure we've collected prints from the latches. It's not likely, but seeing as how there are two sets of gates, we might get lucky."

I waited to see if my husband was done. I didn't want to derail him. If he had more information to share, I hoped to hear it. But when he paused to take a long drink from his coffee cup, I told him what I'd learned the night before.

CHAPTER 13

"My customers had a lot to say about the murder in the dog park. They knew Archie Wellington, and he was not a popular guy."

Detweiler nodded. "News of the victim's identity traveled fast."

I explained about Mabel Henderson's mother watching the whole drama unfold through binoculars from a nearby sixth floor perch. Detweiler and I both chuckled about that.

"Who needs cable when they have a good pair of binoculars?" he joked.

"Naturally, given Mabel's mother's on-the-spot reporting, my customers chewed my ear off about Archie Wellington. I asked them if I could share with you, and they said go ahead."

Detweiler grinned. "Time in a Bottle isn't exactly a sacred confessional. Or is it?"

A rush of blood warmed my face. "Of course, not. That said, it's only fair that I ask my guests for their permission before sharing information with you, isn't it?"

Without a word, Detweiler pulled me close, causing the kitchen chairs to squeak along the floor. After planting a kiss on my cheek, he said, "One of your most endearing qualities is your concern for other people. Anyone else would rationalize and promptly tell me everything. After all, they spoke to you, knowing you're married to a cop, and so they had to take their chances. But you safeguarded their trust in you."

I hugged him and sat upright. "In this instance, keeping my mouth shut would have been trickier than you might guess. Turns out Theresa's daughter Jenny has gathered a lot of rather damning information. It may or may not have to do with the dead body in the dog park, but it sure is inflammatory. I don't think Jenny plans to sit on what she's learned forever."

I explained about the discrepancy between the number of animals put to sleep and the resulting carcasses. "Jenny actually did her own stake-out. She followed a van loaded with animals to a research facility."

Detweiler's face darkened. I'd seen that look before. He wasn't angry. He was livid. "What a stupid chance to take. That girl could have gotten herself killed!"

"You're more right than you know. Jenny talked to her supervisor who told Wellington, and he threatened Jenny," I said with a shiver. Anya could have found herself in the same situation. Both were young women who still believed in fairness, truth triumphing over lies, and all those other fables that time on earth systematically destroys.

"Threatening a young woman. As if shipping animals to a research lab wasn't low enough," Detweiler grumbled. I could hear the cartilage popping in his jaw as he clenched his teeth. Our dentist had made him a bite splint to wear at night, but during the day, he had no relief.

Running a hand through his hair, my husband sighed. "Throw another log on the fire. There seems to be no shortage of people with motives in this case. Mr. Wellington was pushing the city to activate all of their early lease amendments. A lot of downtown retailers would have been given the boot. As you know, moving a business is tricky and costly."

"What do you mean by early lease amendments." I got up and brought the cafetiere of coffee to the table.

"Five years ago, when lease renewals came up, renters were offered a hefty discount if they signed an amendment that gives the city ninety days to end a lease. In public, the city explained they might want to redevelop Main Street at a future date. In private, they assured renters that wasn't likely to happen as no such funds were available." Detweiler shook his head before he sipped his fresh coffee. "I bet you can guess who was behind those lease amendments."

"Archie Wellington?"

"Bingo."

Detweiler got up and poured the dregs of his coffee into the sink. Extending his hand, he silently asked me to hand over my mug, which I did. He rinsed out both cups and swished the dish brush around to clean them.

"Mr. Wellington convinced the city council such an amendment would be important, if a developer came forward with money and plans. What they didn't know was Mr. Wellington already had drawn up plans and found an angel investor. In other words, he played them. Over the years, he seeded the council with his own minions. So much so that his group of pals could easily swing a vote in any direction. At their last shade meeting, they discussed how to present the project and subsequent lease terminations to renters."

"What's a shade meeting?" I picked up the sugar bowl and carried it to the cabinet.

"A non-public meeting. A gathering designed to evade the sunshine laws by allowing elected officials to talk to each other in secret. Supposedly, shade meetings can only take place if there's a compelling legal issue, but Mr. Wellington seems to have presented the city council with exactly that."

If the meeting had been public, there could have been a loud outcry. But done in secret? Everything associated with Archie Wellington smacked of devious and deceitful behavior. Detweiler was working with a plethora of possible suspects.

As if reading my mind, my husband turned, leaned against the counter, and folded his arms over his chest. "Of course, some scuttlebutt about the meeting leaked out, but the council kept most of it under wraps."

"That proposal is only one reason people hated him," I said. "According to my customers, for years now, Wellington has been loud and public about one thing: His nearly pathological distaste for animals."

I told Detweiler what the ladies had said about Wellington's push for dog poop penalties and the quick neutering of animals at the pound. As if she knew what I was saying, Gracie wandered over and leaned against Detweiler. I might be the one who adopted her, but Detweiler is the love of her life. My husband's hand reached down to stroke Gracie's ears.

"Hmm," said Detweiler. "Maybe Mr. Wellington's very public and very loud complaints about animals served another purpose. Maybe he created a smoke screen. While everyone was busy tussling with him over dog poop and neutering strays, Mr. Wellington was working a long game to push through a big redevelopment project worth millions."

Thinking back to Mabel's comment, I couldn't help but agree. Webster Groves was a quiet suburb, a pocket of highly educated citizens, within a park-like area of tree-lined streets, and blessed with housing available at a variety of income levels. Mr. Wellington's proposed changes would definitely reshape our small city.

"Then where do you begin?" I asked. "How will you track

down the person who slipped Mr. Wellington the Ambien? The person who did it must be his killer."

Detweiler gathered me into his arms, and I slipped mine around his waist. Gracie reluctantly moved over to make room for me. "We talk to the baristas and try to track down the person who dosed the drink. We look for more CCTV, hoping we'll get a better picture of people in and out of the café. Then we'll track those people down. We'll interview the various business owners who might have been told their leases were expiring early. They would certainly have a beef with the man."

"What do you know about his personal life?" I asked.

"Not much. Not yet, at least. He inherited his wealth. He was divorced. He owned a house around the corner from the dog park. That's about it so far."

I looked up into those beautiful green eyes I love so much. Since we'd been together, he's slowly accumulated crow's feet, and I find them adorable. "There has to be a reason Wellington's body was left in the dog park. Maybe even a reason his hand was missing."

Detweiler squeezed my fingers together tightly before planting a kiss in my palm. "I think you're right. In fact, I'm sure you're right. I'll know more when I get the medical examiner's report."

CHAPTER 14

I had given Clancy and Nona the day off to go to a craft fair in East St. Louis. It was sort of a busman's holiday, as they'd both been instructed to come back with new products and ideas. They were riding across the river together so they could coordinate their scouting efforts. How different they were from each other! Clancy is all sharp-angles and precision. Nona is like a cloud wafting by.

I hoped they wouldn't kill each other. They are prone to energetic disagreements.

On her way out the door, Clancy wiped at her nose and clucked her tongue at me. "You really need at least one more warm body to help cover our store hours. Honestly, Kiki. This skeletal crew is getting old."

"Yeah, yeah," I said, "I know it. Let me figure out what to do."

Nona gave me one of her Mona Lisa smiles. "Send up a flare. When you ask, the Universe sends answers."

I nodded at her as she left the shop. Nona was right: I needed to hire more help. But at this moment, I didn't have time for vetting a new hire. Not when today was destined to be another long workday.

A constant stream of guests flowed in and out for the next hour. Finally, the store emptied, and I could grab a cup of coffee. The bell over the door chimed and Tangela walked in, carrying her crafting tote bag and a paper coffee cup with a blue flower on the wrapper.

"Hey," she said, not quite meeting my eyes. "Got time to help me with a layout?"

"Sure," I said, leading her to the crop table. Gracie lifted her head as we walked by, but Tangela didn't stop to acknowledge my pup.

I asked, "What are you working on?"

Tangela pulled out several sheets of cardstock and what looked like an old photo album. "I'm finally getting around to making a memorial album. For Beau."

"Beau?" I repeated.

Tangela carefully extracted a photograph from its yellowing sleeve. A magnificent black-and-tan Doberman stared at the camera, alert and proud. Underneath someone had written in pencil "Beau."

"He was beautiful," I said sincerely.

Tangela's eyes misted over. "He was my protector. My everything." She traced the edge of the photo with her finger. "Beau was a retired guard dog. His training never really left him. He was intensely protective. Especially for a male."

Females are often passed over for law enforcement work. If the dog handler went down or was injured, a protective bitch might stay with her person rather than chase a bad guy.

What followed from the sleeve was a series of photos, showing the handsome animal in a range of settings. In one, he sat under a Christmas tree with a Santa's hat on his head. In another, he rested his chin on a stuffed toy, Lamb Chop, a variation of the hand puppet created by Shari Lewis. As the poses changed, Beau stared intently at the photographer. In several, he stood by Tangela's side, his eyes watchful and his powerful body coiled for action. Yes, he was a little scary, but my heart melted at the obvious bond between him and his mistress.

The store phone rang, and I excused myself to answer it. While I was dealing with a customer's question about upcoming classes, I saw Tangela head to the restroom, leaving her materials spread across the work surface.

I shouldn't have looked. Really, I shouldn't have. But something compelled me to glance at the journaling she'd already completed:

Beau came to me after retiring from Sentinel Security Service. The trainer said he was too aggressive for guard work—he'd actually put a man in the hospital for threatening his handler. With me, he was always gentle. Unless he thought I was in danger. Like when someone raised his voice to me. Then nothing could stop Beau...

The bathroom door opened, and I quickly stepped away from the table. Tangela hurried over and gathered up her papers, sliding them into a protective pouch with unusual haste.

"Listen," she said, suddenly. "I wanted to apologize for being short with you yesterday. When you called, I was still upset from everything that happened at the dog park."

"Of course," I said. "Anyone would be. I was, too."

Trembling slightly, she fumbled with her coffee cup. "Right. Thanks for understanding."

She quickly packed up her supplies. "I should go. I'm not in the right mood for crafting after all."

As I watched her hurry out, I couldn't shake the feeling that something was bugging her. Something above and beyond the shock of finding a stray hand and a dead body in the dog park. I'd expected us to talk about that awful morning and the ongoing investigation. Social scientists have proven that women feel better when they talk about a problem, and men feel worse.

Nothing regarding this situation was happening as expected.

CHAPTER 15

After Tangela's odd visit, I needed to clear my head. Gracie came over and pawed my arm as I sat at the projects table, unable to concentrate. She looked at me balefully.

Gracie couldn't have her usual treats anymore, but the vet had approved low-calorie dog yummies. Such treats had to be out there. The challenge was to find them. Since my plans for us to visit the dog park regularly had fallen by the wayside, I made it my new mission to find acceptable treats for Gracie. At the very least, I could buy her a new toy. Call it a sop to my sense of guilt.

Paws & Claws was across the alley from Time in a Bottle. I put a "Back in Fifteen Minutes" sign in the door and we headed over.

Gracie fairly lit up as we walked in. She was eager to sniff around. Neat shelves of supplies and a wall crammed full of offerings ran around the perimeter of the sales floor. In the middle sat a cardboard "dump," a large display unit. This one was filled with dog toys, including stuffed versions of the same Lamb Chop toy Beau had loved, in a wide range of sizes. The largest toys were nearly the size of a real lamb. Gracie's tail wagged slowly as a whimper started in her throat. That was her way of telling me she would like to have a Lamb Chop toy of her own.

Pushing the toys aside, I made my way through the sizes until I found the largest iteration. This I showed Gracie. She exhibited great restraint by only sniffing the toy, but her tail was doing a happy dance.

"Do you like it, sweet girl?"

Her ears pricked up, and her eyes brightened with interest.

"I take that as a yes," I said, tucking the toy under my arm. I looked around for help. A woman in her fifties straightened from stocking a bottom shelf. She was wearing a purple polo shirt with the store logo. Slowly, she got to her feet.

"Welcome to Paws & Claws. I'm Joyce Rivers. Can I help you find anything?"

Gosh, but she looked familiar. I couldn't imagine where we'd met before.

"Do you have any low calorie treats I can feed my Great Dane?" I asked, studying her. Then it hit me: This was the person in the Community Center photo who'd caught that big catfish. My gaze was drawn to an unusual silver necklace she wore. From it dangled a pendant of a dog paw print. The piece caught the light and shone.

"We like Zuke's Mini Naturals Dog Treats. Healthy ingredients and only two calories each," said the clerk, handing me a packet. "Let me give you a tip. Make sure you close the package tightly after it's open. Otherwise, the treats can get hard."

"I'll take them," I said.

Joyce grabbed a bag for me and we headed toward the counter.

"That's a beautiful pendant you're wearing," I said

Her hand flew to her throat, her expression softening.

"Thank you. It's a miniature of Sophie's paw print. My Bernese Swiss Mountain Dog, Sophie. She was..."

Joyce choked up. Blindly, she reached for a box of tissues under the counter. Once she'd mopped her eyes, she said, "Sophie was special."

Gracie responded to the outpouring of emotion by standing on her hind feet and resting her front paws on the counter across from Joyce.

"Down!" I said sternly, but my dog was looking eye-to-eye with Joyce when the woman stretched out a hand to pat Gracie.

"Aren't you a pretty girl?" Joyce cooed to my fur baby as she rubbed behind the dog's ears.

Gracie wagged her tail slowly. Cautiously, she licked Joyce's tears. My dog has always been empathetic, and this was a sterling display of her sweet nature. Joyce's face softened with happiness.

"Sophie was special? Past tense?" I asked gently.

Joyce looked away quickly, dodging my question. Her timing was perfect, because the wall phone rang. As she reached for the receiver with one hand, the other clutched her necklace. She held on to the charm like it was a lifeline to something lost—and it probably was.

While Joyce was occupied with her caller, I browsed a little more, carrying around the stuffed Lamb Chop and following Gracie's lead as she explored. A framed newspaper article caught my eye. Beneath a photo was a caption explaining this was a picture of dog lovers, dog walkers, dog owners, and their pets at a protest rally. Squinting, I could see signs that read, "Keep Webster Groves a dog-friendly community." The ringleader was identified as Bobby Mercato, the owner of this store. Joyce stood off to one side.

"That's an interesting photo," I said, moving back to the front counter when Joyce finished her call. "Looks like this cause has a lot of support."

Joyce nodded. "My boss, Bobby Mercato, has a huge mailing list. When Archie Wellington started harassing dog owners and proposing $500 fines for when pets soil the sidewalks, Bobby pushed back. He emailed customers and convinced them to make their protests clear."

"Did it work?

"Yes and no," said Joyce. "There's still a fine, but it's more reasonable than originally proposed. As to the status of animals in our shelter, that's another story. Remains to be seen if the draconian measures Archie Wellington rammed through the city council will stay in place. There has to be a happy medium."

I concurred. "Not everyone is a pet lover. We all need to live together."

"Our nation has a serious over-population problem with animals," said Joyce. "It falls upon municipalities to do what responsible pet owners refuse to do. That means some animals will need to be sterilized and some will, unfortunately, be euthanized. We can't have packs of wild animals roaming the streets."

We were both silent, remembering the tragedy that happened back in 2001. A pack of dogs had attacked and killed a fourth-grade boy here in St. Louis.

"It's really sad," concluded Joyce, her face closing down with the gravity of our topic. "But there has to be a middle ground."

"One reason I enjoy living here is how nice our neighbors are. Pet-friendly, too." With that, I extended my hand and introduced myself.

Joyce stumbled over my double-barrel last name.

"Call me Kiki," I suggested.

"You own that craft shop, right?" Joyce cocked her head at me. "The one with the parking spaces right across the alley?"

"Yup, I'm the culprit. You'll have to come visit me sometime.

In fact, I'm thinking about offering a special class on memorializing our pets." Actually, the idea had come to me all at once while standing there.

"I bet our customers would be interested in that," said Joyce, and again, her hand went to her pendant. "I know I would. In fact, let me talk to Bobby. Maybe we can put together a promotion. Something to benefit both of us and our customers."

"Sounds perfect!" I said. "Do you have a list of pet parents who've lost their fur babies?"

Joyce's eyes grew damp with tears. "Not per se. However, I know a lot of grieving pet owners."

As if to show her empathy, Gracie again propped her front feet on the counter and nuzzled Joyce.

"Gracie really likes you," I said. Of course, Gracie likes almost everybody, but she really seemed to feel a kinship with Joyce.

"She's wonderful," said Joyce. "Just magnificent." Leaning toward me, Joyce spoke in a hush. "Kiki? Whatever you do, don't let Gracie go outside without you. Even if you have a fenced-in yard."

"What?" This seemed like a strange warning to me. Of course, we don't let Gracie roam free, but why worry about her if she's inside a fenced yard?

Joyce drew in a shuddering breath. "There are creeps out there who snatch dogs from their own yards. They sell the kidnapped dogs to research facilities. It happens more than you'd think. It's a multi-million-dollar black market business."

I felt my jaw drop. I was ready to sputter a question, but a bell rang over the door. A man and woman came in, chatting happily and going immediately to the dog collar section.

Joyce stiffened and reclaimed a sense of professional detachment. "Will that be all? Only the treats? Or would you like to buy the Lamb Chop, too? Did you know this is the most popular dog toy in the country right now?"

"Yes, I'll take the Lamb Chop, too, and no, I didn't know it was that popular." Taking the toy out from under my arm so Joyce could scan the bar code, I was determined to milk this opportunity a little longer. This clerk was clearly a great source of information. As she rang up the items, I whispered, "Joyce? Did you know Archie Wellington? The man whose body they found in the park?"

The change in Joyce was subtle, but unmistakable. Her fingers tightened into knots, knuckles whitening. Her face was neutral, but her voice was brittle. "We had met. Once or twice."

After that, she wouldn't look me in the eye. She handed me a receipt with my total. I paid it and left. Something about Joyce's reaction seemed off. Was she simply choked up with emotion? Or was something else going on? Something involving the protest group? Was it possible one of the protesters had killed Archie Wellington?

Curiouser and curiouser.

On the way back to Time in a Bottle, I couldn't stop thinking about my two strange encounters. There'd been Tangela's odd behavior and Joyce's obvious distress. Were the two connected? Did Tangela know Joyce and vice versa?

CHAPTER 16

I phoned Detweiler, wanting to know if he'd read the statement Tangela had made when we discovered Archie Wellington's body. If so, could he share it with me? Was it possible that Tangela had remembered or reported something I'd overlooked? Living with a homicide detective had taught me a lot about human memory. It's fickle. Memories can bubble up at the most unexpected times. Often, a stray bit of information will shake loose a memory. Even a tiny detail can crack a case.

As it happened, my husband was too busy to talk. But he promised to get back to me when he could. As we said goodbye, I wondered what he'd learned from the medical examiner. What exactly had been Archie Wellington's cause of death? Had his hand been removed before or after he died?

The store was quiet, so I set about my never-ending chore, straightening and restocking shelves. Unfortunately, I made little progress. I seemed to wander around in circles. When my phone chimed and displayed Detweiler's number, I felt a wash of relief. He always makes me feel better. For the duration of our call, I could listen to him and get my wits about me. At this rate, I wasn't doing my shop any good.

"Medical examiner's report is in," he said grimly. "Cause of death was blunt force trauma to the head," said Detweiler. "The hand was ripped off by an animal. But here's where it gets interesting. They found fragments of lead pellets embedded in the head wound. The ME thinks the murder weapon was a homemade sap.

"There's more," he said. "They found healed defensive wounds on the victim's hand. These would have needed stitches. That's the same hand that was severed. I'm thinking the killer wanted to make a statement, and he used that hand as a message. It wasn't a random injury. Those old wounds were dog bites."

CHAPTER 17

Saturday morning dawned bright and shiny. Brawny and I had promised to take the boys to the Science Center, one of St. Louis's most fascinating destinations. Anya was meeting friends to shop and watch a movie at the cineplex in the mall, which meant she wouldn't get home until late. Detweiler left me a note on our bedside table saying he loved me and hoped to get off early that evening. I folded and tucked it into my pocket before waking up the boys.

Somehow, we'd never visited the free museum and planetarium in the time since Ty had been born. It was one of those cases when you live in a place and you shove the vaunted tourist sites to the back of your mind. After all, they're in your backyard and you can visit them any time, right? Except you don't. You keep postponing the trip.

This visit would be epic because Ty loves dinosaurs, and the Science Center boasts a life-sized animatronic Tyrannosaurus rex, complete with a blood-chilling roar. I was as excited as the boys were about seeing this spectacle in action.

We almost made it out the front door when my phone lit up

with Clancy's number. Her voice was so low and croaky I could barely make out her words. "Caught a cold. Can't breathe. Can't think. Need to stay in bed," she said. "Sorry."

I told Brawny about Clancy's ailment. "Looks like I have to tend to the store."

"Aye, and I'll drop off a quart of chicken noodle soup for Clancy on our way to the Science Center," said the nanny.

"That's a good idea," I agreed.

As the kids drove off with Brawny, I waved from the front window and fought the urge to whine. Clancy is rarely sick, and she's always dependable. Sure, her timing stunk, but I reminded myself, "It is what it is." There was nothing to do but take her shift at the store.

Because the morning had dawned so fine, there were very few customers. They drifted in and out, like the dogwood blossoms would when they fell from the trees. In a way, the pace was perfect. There was enough human interaction to keep me mentally occupied and enough slack time so I didn't feel rushed off my feet.

It came as a relief not to think about the dead body in the dog park.

Around three, I looked up from a project and came face-to-face with Joyce from Paws & Claws. Dressed in a colorful striped sweater that made her look like a LEGO toy, the woman tossed down a folder and pulled up a stool at my craft table. Giving the shop an appreciative once-over, Joyce grinned. "Cool place!"

Seeing her new friend, Gracie rose from her dog bed and ambled over, giving Joyce the equivalent of a soulful doggy grin. The two indulged in a love fest while I kept working, prepping for a St. Patrick's Day class. I like to get everything done before the announcement of an offering goes out via email.

As soon as Joyce and Gracie were tired of sharing affection, my guest turned to me and asked, "Is this a good time?" When I nodded, she barreled on, talking a mile a minute.

"I took the liberty of contacting another sponsor for your class. Dr. Ellen Blackman runs counseling sessions for grieving pet owners. She's always looking for healthy ways for people to channel their emotions. Like the pendant I'm wearing. The one you noticed. I hope you don't mind me talking to her."

Of course, I didn't mind. Instantly, I recalled seeing the doctor's name in that puff piece Tangela had shown me about the dog park. I love bringing people into a project. Variety is like rocket fuel for creativity.

Now that we'd moved past our initial hurdles, Joyce and I got down to the hard work of planning a special event. She was pleasantly surprised when I brought out our project planning guide, a heuristic device we keep perfecting. In almost no time at all, we'd outlined the offerings, listed possible dates and costs, and strategized ways to make the event a success. As we were wrapping up, I asked Joyce a question that had been bugging me.

"I saw the picture of you holding up that big catfish. But you didn't seem overly happy with the award," I said.

"Pffftt," sputtered Joyce. A non-response response if there ever was one. "I hated noodling. Hated it. I only went because my father and brothers are keen fishermen. They badgered me into it. In the end, it took less effort to go with them than to keep dodging their invitations. The boys in my family gang up on me because I'm the only girl. Once we got to the riverbank, I decided I'd show them a thing or two."

"Isn't it creepy? Sticking your hand down in a hole and wiggling your fingers? Scares me to think about it," I said as I made photocopies of the email lists of pet owners she'd brought along. They would need to be inputted, which was a tedious process, but adding these contacts was a bonus. Ever since

Covid, I've come to realize that being able to communicate directly with your customers is a high priority.

Joyce's entire face closed up, like an invisible hand had rolled down window shades. "Compared to what followed that weekend, getting bitten by a catfish wasn't a big deal."

Now I was totally confused. Looked to me like "what followed" was winning a competition. Yet Joyce implied the next step was a negative experience. In fact, her whole demeanor turned despondent.

I did what we always do at Time in a Bottle when a person obviously needs to hit the re-set button. From the refrigerator, I grabbed a cold bottle of Diet Dr Pepper and set it in front of Joyce. She opened it and took a long swallow. "That weekend, I left Sophie with a dog-sitter," she said, slowly mastering her emotions. "When I got home, I found out my dog had run off. Slipped her leash and vanished. It took me weeks to find out where she'd gone. By then, she'd been sold to a research facility in a pound seizure operation."

"A what?" I could barely choke out the words

Joyce fortified herself with another long swallow of Diet Dr Pepper. "In the past three years, laboratories have used 44,000 cats and dogs for experiments. Tens of thousands of puppies are purpose-bred and go directly to research facilities, so they aren't counted in that number. In some states, if a lab needs more animals for their work, they can activate a process called a 'pound seizure', which requires the shelter to turn over animals when requested. Missouri has no restrictions that stop this sort of exchange." Joyce paused. She looked away until she got herself under control.

Starting again, she said, "Of course, the shelters claim they check all pets for micro-chips and tags and whatnot, but do they? Who knows? Sophie was micro-chipped and wore a collar with tags. Even so, I wasn't notified when she was picked up. In fact, it took a lot of detective work to track her down."

This explanation hit me like a punch to the gut. I couldn't even form words or thoughts. The very idea of a profit-making concern swooping in and herding defenseless animals into a van, taking them to be tortured, and eventually killed in the name of science, was beyond horrifying.

"How on earth did you learn what happened to Sophie?" I had one hand on Gracie's neck. She'd head-butted me for attention when she noticed how upset I'd gotten.

"A group of college kids, members of PETA—People for the Ethical Treatment of Animals—hacked into the databases of several Missouri animal shelters. Once there, they found lists of research facilities. They followed the breadcrumbs and hacked into the research facilities, although as you might guess, that took a lot more time. Eventually, their efforts were rewarded. They found a motherlode of files listing animals the labs purchased. Often, the intake person made notes on the animal's appearance and any distinguishing marks, particularly the breed and the weight. Always, the files included the date the animal was acquired and the geographic area it came from."

I couldn't breathe. In a way, all of this made sense. It wasn't much different from how I unboxed supplies. You had to record your raw materials and costs or you couldn't lay claim to any sort of quality control. But doing this with an animal? Outrage and sorrow went to war within me.

"The hackers used AI to compare the lists. They had a hunch that not all the dogs were sourced properly. And they were right." Joyce covered her face with her large, rough hands. She scrubbed at her face, leaving her skin red and raw. "Sophie's disappearance matched records from the lists, the shelters' documents, and the purchase details from one lab. She couldn't have been at the pound for more than 48 hours. Of course, she was micro-chipped. And yes, she had a collar with tags. But that didn't matter. I tried to get an attorney to represent me, but I was too late."

For a few minutes, we sat there in silence. Finally, she said, "That's why I warned you about someone scooping up Gracie. I suspect that large dogs, ones that weigh nearly as much as a person, might be especially desirable for research purposes."

CHAPTER 18

Sunday morning while we were still in bed, I told Detweiler what I'd learned about pound seizures. He was as appalled as I was. I couldn't get over what had happened to Sophie. I explained to my husband how I'd come to know more about Joyce, after seeing her photo at the community center. How she'd been out of town, and how that led to Sophie running off. Then, tragically, how the sweet dog had been sold to a research facility.

"It's ridiculous!" I said. "Sophie was micro-chipped. She had on a collar with tags when she ran off. Joyce was only out of contact for a weekend, and yet, that was long enough for them to sell her dog. Worst of all, it was perfectly legal."

I was horrified to learn that Missouri treated shelter animals in such a cavalier manner. After babbling on and on, I finally wore myself out. Detweiler gave me a long hug before getting dressed for work and going into the station. Lately, it seemed like he was working seven days a week. Our home life suffered when he was hit with a lot of investigations all at once. Usually, I'm okay with his hours, but today, it really bothered me. After he left, I took a long hot shower and tried to compartmentalize.

If I'd let myself, I would have crawled back under the covers and spent the whole day in bed. But that wouldn't bring back Sophie or any of the other animals who'd been treated with such cruelty.

Besides, I had children who depended on me, and they would be up and about any minute. Brawny had the day off. Anya had asked to spend the night with a friend, so she wasn't home. That left me and my boys. No way was I going to let them see me so downcast. The Littles, our nickname for Erik and Ty, wouldn't understand what was making me sad. I needed to dig deep and find a wholesome activity for us to share.

I was dressed when Clancy messaged to say she was still sick. She was running a fever, and she wasn't coming into Time in a Bottle because she didn't want to spread her germs. That was fine by me. Once we get any sort of contagious illness started in our family, it makes the rounds until we're all sick. I texted Clancy that she was doing the right thing. I knew better than to contact Nona. Every third Sunday she gets together with a group of women called the Miss Fits, and they work to improve their psychic abilities. The long and short of it was that I needed to go into work—and I would have to take the boys with me.

"Guess what?" I said. "Today is a special day for you two. You get to come to work with me!"

They gave each other a sideways glance. Smart little rascals. They were immediately suspicious of my enthusiasm.

"Brawny?" asked Ty, cautiously. Admittedly, she's a lot more fun than I am, especially when I'm at my store.

"She has the day off. She told me you tuckered her out. I guess the Tyrannosaurus rex at the Science Museum was totally awesome, right?" I tried to project as much gaiety into my voice as possible.

"I want to adopt a cockroach." Erik folded his hands over his chest. "I've been very, very good and my birthday is coming up."

I knew exactly what he was talking about. The Science Center has a hands-on, kids' area that features Madagascar Hissing Cockroaches. Just my luck, these appealed to my oldest son. Was he frightened of bugs? No, not in the least.

Was I?

No, but there's a Grand Canyon-sized gap between appreciating a two-inch cockroach inside a glass display case and having one take up residence in your home. That gulf was the metaphorical "bridge too far" for me. Nevertheless, I kept the sunny smile on my face.

"We'll have to see about that. In the meantime, I thought that maybe the two of you would like to decorate my store with new pictures of dinosaurs and animals and bugs. Cockroaches. Whatever. But only after we go to Perkins for pancakes."

Okay, that got their attention. Nothing like a big lake of maple syrup and a bite-size portion of pancake to start a guy's day. Although they were sticky, both boys were in a terrific mood by the time we pulled into my parking lot. Next to a police cruiser. A Webster Groves police cruiser.

That's when a really, really big cockroach stumbled out in front of us. Officer Randall hoisted his pants and his utility belt and waddled my way. "Mrs. Lo-Det-way-leer. I need to see you down at the station. Right now. We need to talk about a piece of a stuffed toy you dumped in the weeds by the dog park."

CHAPTER 19

"The boys stay with me," I said firmly, though my heart was racing. I had no idea what Officer Randall was talking about. Erik clutched my left hand while Ty grabbed my right.

"Fine." Officer Randall shrugged, clearly enjoying my discomfort. "I take it you know the way? I'll follow."

The drive to the station was a blur. The stuffed toy I'd dropped in the weeds? It didn't exist. What on earth was Officer Randall talking about? Yes, I'd bought Gracie a stuffed toy, but that was after my visit to the dog park. How could this cop link this new find with me? It made little sense. In my rearview mirror, I could see Officer Randall's cruiser. He drove so close he was practically in my backseat. The boys were unusually quiet.

"Mommy?" Ty's voice quavered. "Are you in trouble?"

"No, sweetheart. This is just a misunderstanding." I hoped I sounded more confident than I felt.

The Webster Groves Police Department occupied an imposing brick building. Officer Randall escorted us through the front doors like we were hardened criminals, one meaty hand gripping my shoulder. Erik and Ty stayed glued to my side.

We'd barely made it to the lobby when a tall woman with silver hair and captain's bars on her uniform emerged from an office. Her sharp eyes took in the scene: me, flanked by two frightened children, with Officer Randall preening behind us.

"What's going on here, Randall?" Her voice could have frozen lava.

"Captain Martinez, I brought in our prime suspect in the Wellington case. She's probably the one who messed with our evidence." He puffed up importantly. "And two material witnesses."

"Material witnesses?" Captain Martinez's eyebrows shot toward her hairline. "Those 'material witnesses' appear to be children. Very young children." Her gaze swept over my boys, noting their sticky faces and rumpled clothes. "Who just had pancakes, if I'm not mistaken?"

Randall's chest deflated slightly. "Well, yes, but—"

"And this would be Mrs. Lowenstein-Detweiler? Detective Detweiler's wife?"

I gave her a little wave of acknowledgement.

"Yes, but—"

"The same Mrs. Lowenstein-Detweiler who already gave a full statement? Who discovered the body with her dog? Who is married to one of the Major Case Squad's senior investigators? A man who's helping us sort out the dog park problem?"

Each question cracked like a whip.

Officer Randall's face had gone from florid to pale. "I thought—"

"No, Officer Randall, you didn't think." Captain Martinez turned to me. "Mrs. Lowenstein-Detweiler, I apologize for this disruption to your Sunday. You and your children are free to go."

"But Captain—" Randall sputtered.

"Officer Randall, my office. Now." Her tone could have stripped paint. "Mrs. Lowenstein-Detweiler, would your boys like some cookies? Officer Theodorus keeps a stash of Oreos in the break room."

I could feel Erik and Ty relaxing their death grips on my hands. "That's very kind, but we should probably head back to my store. Actually, I should have opened an hour ago."

"Of course." She smiled warmly at the boys, then turned that smile into a glare as she focused on Randall. "Officer, I'm still waiting."

As we walked out, I could hear her voice rising: "What were you thinking, dragging in children without a parent's counsel present? Do you want to get us sued?"

The rest faded as the door closed behind us. In the car, Ty asked, "Mommy, why was that lady police officer so mad at the other police officer?"

"Because, sweetie, sometimes people get so focused on looking important that they forget to do what's right."

The boys seemed to accept this. As we drove to Time in a Bottle, I called Detweiler. He needed to know about Officer Randall's latest power play. The boys were settled at a low table with their coloring books when Detweiler burst through the front door of Time in a Bottle. His face was thunderous.

"I can't believe what Randall did," he said, pulling me aside. "But there's more to it than meets the eye. You won't believe what that idiot was trying to cover up."

I raised my eyebrows. "Cover up?"

"Remember how Officer Randall was first on scene at the dog park? Turns out he did a half-baked job securing the perimeter. I sent in a second forensics team yesterday, and they discovered what sloppy work he'd done. In fact, they found two items he missed."

Detweiler's jaw clenched as he continued, "One was a leg of lamb."

"What?" In my mind, I pictured a piece of meat, bone intact.

As I pondered this, Ty's Crayola marker rolled onto the floor. I swooped down and grabbed it.

Detweiler cleared things up. "A portion of a stuffed toy sheep like what you bought for Gracie."

He went on, "The second item was a plastic baggy filled with small weights. It had been tossed into some weeds outside the dog park fence. It was ripped open and a few of the pellets had fallen out."

My hand flew to my mouth. "That must have been the murder weapon!"

"The lab confirmed it. A spatter of Mr. Wellington's blood was on a small section of the bag."

"So Officer Randall..." I began.

"Hauled you in to deflect attention from his sloppy police work. He'd gotten the news from the crime scene team before we did, and he knew he'd messed up. His default position was to point a finger at you, instead of admitting he'd missed crucial evidence." Detweiler ran a hand through his hair. "Captain Martinez is furious and I am, too. The leg from the stuffed toy and the plastic bag sat there for at least a day after Mr. Wellington's body was found. Those items were exposed to the elements. We're lucky the lab could get anything useful from the bag."

"Wow," I said. "What a jerk! And to pull that stunt in front of the boys."

"No kidding," snarled Detweiler. "Are they okay?"

"I think so." I began haltingly. "About that stuffed animal... Joyce told me Lamb Chop is the most popular dog toy in the country. While it's possible the piece came from Paws & Claws, it could have come from a lot of places."

"Good to know," said Detweiler.

"About those weights you found," I said slowly. "Remember, I told you about Joyce belonging to a family of keen fishermen? I bet she has all sorts of bait and tackle—"

"And lead weights." Detweiler jumped ahead. He was already pulling out his phone. "This could be the connection we needed. But first, I need to deal with Officer Randall. No one drags my wife and kids to a police station to cover their own incompetence. I promised Captain Martinez I'd drop by the Webster Groves Police Department so we could discuss the matter."

CHAPTER 20

After saying goodbye to Detweiler, I couldn't stop thinking about the photo I'd seen at Paws & Claws, the picture of Richard Montgomery at the protest rally. Hadn't someone said his wife owned Rottweilers?

Did that matter?

The boys were working at a kid-sized table with watercolors, markers, and big pieces of newsprint so they could color to their hearts' content. I pulled up the local newspaper's website on my phone and searched for Richard Montgomery's name. The results surprised me.

"Champion Rottweiler Neutered by Mistake at Local Pound" screamed a headline from eight months ago. The article detailed how Richard Montgomery had accidentally left his back door unlocked. A nearby poodle was in heat. In a frenzied bid for a romantic encounter, the Montgomerys' prized Rottweiler, Zeus, had gotten out. Before dawn, animal control had picked Zeus up. Thanks to the immediate neutering policy, Zeus was altered before Richard or his wife, MaryBeth, could retrieve their valuable pet.

I knew exactly who had pushed through that policy: Archie Wellington.

The ramifications of Richard's lapse in judgment had been devastating. Zeus could no longer compete or be used for breeding. His entire career as a show dog had been destroyed in one quick procedure. MaryBeth Montgomery had been quoted saying, "This is an outrage. Zeus was clearly well-cared for, wore tags, and was micro-chipped. There was no reason for the animal shelter to rush him into surgery without attempting to contact us first."

Two months later, the same newspaper ran a small piece about their divorce. MaryBeth had cited Richard's "negligence and irresponsible behavior" as contributing factors. I switched to the website of a local weekly shopper. A "Your Neighbors" column inside explained the Montgomerys were awarded divided custody of their dogs. MaryBeth had moved to Chicago to start fresh, taking Zeus with her. Richard was keeping Zeus's littermate, Zena, as a pet.

I remembered Lulu talking about Richard at craft night: "A good egg, but kind of a dim bulb." Now I understood what she meant. His carelessness had cost him his marriage and destroyed his wife's champion breeding program.

Wellington had been the architect of the policy that made it all go wrong.

I made a mental note to mention this to Detweiler. Richard Montgomery definitely had a strong motive to want to see Archie Wellington dead.

A customer walked in, distracting me from my thoughts.

CHAPTER 21

Five o'clock finally came. I flipped the sign in the front door to CLOSED. I wanted to shout, "Hallelujah!" and race out of the building. The boys had colored for a short interval, gotten bored and whined away the rest of the afternoon. I couldn't blame them. As a special treat, I ordered a pizza for our dinner and had it delivered to the house. We were back home, eating at the kitchen table, when my husband phoned to say his estimated time of arrival was within the hour. Brawny was more than happy to get the Littles ready for bed, and I promised to read to them once they were snug as bugs.

Both boys were splashing around in the bathroom upstairs when the doorbell rang. I couldn't identify the visitor, but it didn't really matter. Gracie was glued to my side. She growled lightly. Although the hood of the navy raincoat was pulled low, the shape of my guest's lips made her easy to identify. Tangela was standing on my doorstep. "May I come in?" she asked.

I hesitated, but I wasn't too worried. Brawny was upstairs with the boys, and Detweiler was on his way home. Anya had called me at work to ask if she could have dinner with her grandparents. If Tangela meant me any harm, she'd have to defend herself from Brawny, Gracie, and Detweiler.

I nodded toward my kitchen. "I'll fix us a cup of tea," I suggested. "Or would you prefer coffee?"

The minute the words were out of my mouth, my brain replayed memories of Morning Glory Café coffee cup wrappers. The first time I'd seen one was when Tangela met me at the dog park. Later, Detweiler told me Archie Wellington's coffee had been dosed at the little restaurant. What's more, CCTV showed a culprit at the café wearing a dark raincoat. Like the one facing me now. My mouth went dry.

Gracie growled

Tangela grabbed me by the elbow. "I'm not here to hurt you. Or your kids. I'm here to explain what happened. I would dearly love a cup of coffee."

The kitchen was quiet, but I could hear the boys chattering about which pajamas to wear. I willed myself to stay calm. "Have a seat, Tangela, I'd like to hear what you have to say. Be forewarned: our nanny has had extensive combat training. She's right upstairs."

"Understood." She pulled a chair closer to the table. Gracie approached her cautiously. "Where is your husband?" she asked.

"I'm expecting him any minute," I lied. Gracie stood between me and my guest. Her hackles were raised.

"Got it." Tangela spread her fingers wide on the tabletop. She said nothing as I filled the cafetiere with fresh ground coffee and turned on the electric kettle. When I sat down across from her, she began, "You've seen photos of Beau, my Doberman. He was very protective. One day I was walking him, and our route took us by those houses that Archie intends to redevelop. He was talking to a permit runner when he mistook me for one of the locals who objected to the project. Planning to give me a piece of his mind, he came roaring over to us, yelling at me, and waving his arms in the air. Before I could stop him, Beau attacked. Grabbed Archie by the hand and pulled him to the ground."

The kettle clicked off. I poured hot water into the cafetiere, but I didn't interrupt Tangela. I was eager to hear more. While she gathered her thoughts, I put cups, spoons, milk, and sugar on the table. After pressing the plunger, I put the cafetiere where she could reach it.

"Beau's bite was bad enough it took a lot of stitches. Archie pressed every available legal lever. After a series of threats, I had no choice but to put Beau to sleep." Tangela broke into a sob. I handed her a stack of paper napkins. "I betrayed that poor dog. He was staring into my eyes when he died by injection. After, I went into a dark spiral. My sisters and my boss were worried about me. My GP gave me Ambien to help me sleep at night. He also wrote a prescription for Dr. Ellen Blackman's grief counseling sessions."

After adding milk and sugar, she stirred her drink. Her spoon made gentle clicking sounds as it bumped the sides of the mug. "At the counseling sessions, I learned what Archie had done to other pet owners. I met Joyce Rivers from Claws & Paws, and Richard Montgomery. He and his wife—now ex-wife—used to breed Rottweilers. Richard still has a Rottie as a pet. At first, we didn't share how our dogs had been impacted by Archie Wellington. Only that we were grieving. Then one day, a young woman came to our meetings and introduced herself. She was Jenny Sanchez. She and a hacker from PETA were doing their best to gather evidence about what Archie was doing. If we would provide her with details about our pets, she'd see if they could trace what happened to specific dogs. Of course, I already knew what had happened to Beau, so I kept my mouth shut. I never intended to share my story. After all, I'm the one who ultimately decided to have Beau put to sleep. As we sat there, Jenny shared some of her research. All of us were astonished by the number of animals disappearing and being sold to research facilities—and I got angry. So did Joyce and Richard."

Tangela took a long slurp of her coffee. "After that, the three of us adults met frequently. Jenny's information was damning, but she couldn't prove Archie was the driving force behind the shelter transfers. Richard pointed out Archie could claim everything was the fault of the city council or the animal shelter. He could always come up with an excuse. The longer we talked, the madder I got. So did Richard. And Joyce. Eventually, we hatched a plan."

Soft murmurs floated down from upstairs. Brawny was reading to the boys. How she'd convinced them to listen to her reading the books rather than hold out for me, was a mystery, but I was thankful for the switch. I feared that if I got up and walked away from Tangela, I'd never hear the whole story.

I offered her more coffee.

Tangela accepted it gratefully. "Richard suggested we corner Archie and try to get him to admit his involvement in various schemes to get rid of pets. Thanks to social media, we could video him and share it with the world. To get him to talk, he'd have to be relaxed, of course, and Archie wasn't a drinker. But I had an idea. I volunteered to dose him with Ambien. I knew Archie had stopped by the Morning Glory Café every morning. I'd seen him there. I figured it would be easy enough to grind Ambien pills into a fine powder and dose his coffee."

I asked, "And then what? Wouldn't the powder make him woozy?"

"Of course, it made him woozy! That was the whole point. It didn't take long, either. Richard and Joyce waited for him outside of the restaurant. Archie made it halfway down the block before his legs nearly gave out. Richard and Joyce braced him. We'd decided the best place for them to confront Archie was in the dog park. Seemed fitting, you know? I watched them frog-march him toward it, and I went back to my car. I sat there with Bailey until it was time for me to meet you."

She sighed. "The minutes went by so slowly. I hated sitting and waiting, but I'd done my part like I promised, and I trusted they would do theirs. I had no idea Archie Wellington would wind up dead!"

"Why are you telling me this?" I asked. My words sounded sharp, but I needed to know her intentions. Was she planning to confess to the police? This was a person I'd hoped would become a friend. Now I found it tough to put up with her. I understood why she'd drugged Archie Wellington, but I was furious she'd let me get caught up in her scheme.

Tangela stared down at a splash of coffee next to her cup. Using a fingertip, she traced it, enlarging the circle. "I'm here for a lot of reasons. First, I feel crummy about dragging you into this. Second, I'm worried about Jenny Sanchez. She's a good kid. The longer this goes on, the more involved she'll be, and she could get hurt. The monsters selling dogs might get violent if their supply of merchandise dries up. And last of all, this needs to be public. Otherwise, another creep like Archie Wellington might take over where he left off."

Tears streamed down her face, and she stared at me. "I'm so, so sorry. I know you can't forgive me right now, but maybe someday in the future?"

CHAPTER 22

Seeing her remorse, I remembered why I'd wanted her as a friend. Originally, my instincts had told me that Tangela was a good person. Maybe she still was. She had messed up, and the consequences had been serious.

The tension of the moment was broken as Detweiler came in through the garage. Although he looked tired and disheveled, his face was alive with curiosity when he saw Tangela. He recognized her from when she was at the dog park. They hadn't formally met, so I introduced them.

"I think you should tell my husband what you told me," I urged her. "But first, let me get all of us more coffee."

While I refilled the cafetiere and set the water boiling, Detweiler pulled out a chair and sat down. Tangela seemed frozen, unsure of how to proceed. My husband eased her along by being conversational.

He said, "I'm late getting home because I met with Jenny Sanchez at her parents' house. What a smart and courageous young lady. She gave me a hard drive with her research and the documentation dug up by the PETA hackers. Somehow, I think it's the tip of the iceberg. Archie Wellington was obsessive with his hatred of animals. He made it his life's mission to destroy people's pets. Especially their dogs. What a sad, miserable excuse for a human being."

Tangela's face contorted with pain. "You do not know how much hurt he inflicted on pet owners. Let me tell you what happened to me..."

CHAPTER 23

Tangela's confession made for a grim evening. Once she was well into it, I left her with my husband. I'd had enough misery for one week. I went upstairs and checked on the Littles before showering and getting ready for bed. I was drying my hair when I heard the front door close, and my husband's footsteps on the treads.

"Tangela's gone home. Can we talk about this tomorrow?" he asked. "I'm exhausted, and I imagine you already know most of what I heard."

The next morning, he roused me with a kiss on the forehead. "It's still early, but could you get dressed and come with me? I think we can get this wrapped up."

After throwing on clothes, I settled into the passenger seat of his cruiser and watched the world go by while he talked. Tangela had told Detweiler what she'd told me. Frankly, I was sick of thinking about the murder in the dog park. I had no sympathy for Archie Wellington. I ached for all those animals sent to research facilities, but my feelings about Tangela were still complicated.

"What are we doing here?" I asked Detweiler as we pulled into the parking lot of Paws & Claws. The unopened store's windows were dark.

"Ms. Rivers contacted the station last night and left a message asking to meet me here this morning," said my husband. "She specifically requested you come along."

Joyce was waiting by the back door, her hand clutching that silver paw print charm. She looked smaller somehow, deflated, like a balloon after losing its air. "Thank you for coming," she said, her voice barely above a whisper. "Richard is on his way."

"Richard Montgomery?" I asked.

She nodded. A dirty gray Camry pulled up. Richard climbed out of his car with his shoulders hunched. We introduced ourselves. He looked nothing like the angry protestor I'd seen in that newspaper photo. Instead of strident, he was broken down.

Joyce led us to the stockroom. There we gathered around a card table. Each of us claimed a metal chair. Joyce made it as far as her seat and collapsed in tears. Richard took another chair and stared off into space.

"It wasn't supposed to happen like this," Joyce said at last, wiping her eyes. Detweiler sat next to me. He had flipped his jacket open, allowing his service weapon to show. If there was going to be trouble, my husband would be ready. But I didn't think there would be. The atmosphere wasn't confrontational. It was sad.

"Tell me more, Ms. Rivers," said Detweiler. "You have our full attention."

"We only wanted Archie to admit what he'd done. How he'd used us and our pets to make money and to distract the city council," she spoke in a rush. "By causing a diversion, he was able to push through a lot of legislation, clearing the way for his redevelopment plans."

"He styled himself as a concerned citizen and a developer who wanted to see Webster Groves thrive," said Richard. "That was never his goal. He used everyone and everything to make money. He made millions selling animals to labs. He wanted to kill as many of our pets as possible. And he didn't care how brutally they were treated at the end of their lives."

"What changed your minds about coming forward?" Detweiler asked quietly. "Why did you ask us to meet you here this morning?"

Joyce threw up her hands. "We had to do something. Late last night, Tangela called and told me she'd confessed her part in this. To both of you, no less. She's prepared to accept the consequences. But that doesn't seem fair. Archie's death wasn't her fault."

"That's one reason," said Richard. "The other is Jenny Sanchez. We're worried that girl is going to get herself killed if you don't intervene. Those jerks who transported pets to labs were making good money. If they blame her, instead of Archie, for messing up their business, she could be in danger."

Detweiler nodded. "Why don't you start at the beginning? That way I can be sure I haven't missed anything."

Richard explained, "The three of us—Tangela, Joyce, and I—met in Dr. Blackman's pet loss support group. All of us hated Archie Wellington. He caused our misery. Me, after Zeus was neutered. Joyce, after Sophie was sold to a laboratory. And Tangela, who was forced to put Beau to sleep."

Joyce said, "One night, we stayed late after our meeting and talked about Archie. That's when we decided to make him confess. We figured we'd video him, and the dog park seemed like the perfect place to do it. We would confront him about his misdeeds. Our goal was to record him bragging about how he was making money by murdering our pets."

Richard continued, "But first, we had to get him into the dog park. Then we needed to loosen him up, get him talking. That's where the Ambien came in. Tangela volunteered her personal stash. She said it would be easy for her to dose his coffee at the café. Archie was a creature of habit. He would get his coffee and walk to his office, a little more than a block away. Our plan was to waylay him after he'd had his coffee and force him to come to the dog park with us."

"That's what we did," said Joyce. "We followed him as he left the café. He'd gone about a block when we could see his legs wobble. Richard took one arm, and I took the other. We pointed him in the direction of the dog park and kept him moving."

Richard gave us a rueful smile. "I was so sure it wouldn't take long to get a confession that I brought along Zena, my Doberman, for a car ride. As you'll recall, it was coolish that day, so I left her in my Volvo with the windows partially down. She was in sight of the dog park."

Joyce rolled her eyes. "Richard underestimated her ability to squirm through small spaces."

"I was concentrating on Archie," said Richard, sounding defensive. "Joyce was using her iPhone to take a video. I was trying to get him to admit all the harm he'd done and all the money he was making off his tricks. But as I'd ask him questions, he would laugh at me. He said we were pathetic. He said we were perverts for loving animals. He bragged about stealing dogs out of people's front yards! He told me how much money he'd made, and I couldn't believe it. Then he made a grab for Joyce's phone. We tussled over it, and he came right after me and nearly knocked me down. I punched him in the face."

Richard hung his head. "I admit I have anger issues. That's what got me into this mess. I got drunk after quarreling with my wife. She stomped out to spend the night in a hotel. I didn't lock our back door, and Zeus got out. Archie not only ruined Zeus, he ruined my marriage as well. I told him I wanted him dead."

Richard wiped his nose on his sleeve and continued, "Archie threw himself at me. Grabbed me by the throat. Zena wormed her way out of the car. She tried to bring him down."

"Archie kicked the dog," said Joyce. "I could hear the Rottweiler's yelps of pain. He kicked her again and again. Neither Richard nor I were armed. In the pocket of my jacket was a bag of lead fishing weights, leftover from my excursion with my brothers. I don't even remember reaching for it. We were all struggling. I was crying. Richard was on the ground, and Archie was on top of him. Zena crawled on her belly, whining in pain. It was awful."

I held my breath. This described a bad situation, spiraling out of control.

Joyce said, "Grabbing the weights wasn't even a conscious decision. But I had to do something. I had to stop Archie! I hit him as hard as I could. You have to understand—I only wanted him to leave Richard and Zena alone. Everything was a blur. When I regained my senses, Archie was dead, and Zena was chewing on his hand."

CHAPTER 24

"What's going to happen to us?" asked Richard.

"I don't know," said Detweiler, and he gave me a look that said, "Thank God sentencing isn't up to me."

I got to my feet, even though I felt light-headed. Dimly, I heard Detweiler talking to dispatch. Several patrol cars would be coming. One would give me a ride home. Detweiler made sure I was buckled in. I put one staying hand on his arm. "What about that leg of lamb you found?"

He smiled. "Despite the fact it looked like a sheep, I believe we can safely assume it was a red herring."

When I frowned, he put a kiss on my forehead. "Babe, I think some other dog lost a part of his or her Lamb Chop stuffed toy. I don't think it had anything to do with this particular crime."

"Oh," I said and slumped back in the seat. Detweiler gave the uniformed officer our address. Thankfully, the man behind the wheel didn't try to strike up a conversation.

This whole mess hit me hard. Good people in pain had

caved into their worst instincts and tragedy followed. It was horrible. Just awful.

Brawny took one look at my tear-streaked face and offered to watch the store. She would drop the kids off at school and go work at Time in a Bottle until Clancy and Nona arrived. I nodded to her gratefully. I was an emotional mess. Visions of innocent dogs being tortured in the name of research compounded the imagined grief of losing Gracie. Flashing images of the severed hand only made everything worse.

How could a playdate at the dog park go so terribly wrong? Thanking Brawny, I went into the main bedroom and cried myself to sleep. Around noon, I woke up, washed my puffy face, called to Gracie, and drove us to my store.

Nona had taped a "Help Wanted" sign in the front window. She took one look at me and squeezed my shoulders with both hands. "You have done everyone a great service, but you certainly paid a high price."

Clancy asked, "Is it over?"

"Yes," I said

"How close were you to figuring everything out?" Clancy arched a brow at me.

I made a seesaw motion with one hand

Brawny patted me on the back. "I have things to do at the house. See you later."

"I'm assuming Richard Montgomery's the one who dealt Archie Wellington the fatal blow?" asked Clancy.

"No, it was Joyce. Her dog Sophie and that pet store were Joyce's entire world. I think she snapped when she heard Paws & Claws would lose its lease."

Clancy shook her head. "I still don't get why Tangela had to get you involved."

"I think the timing of me wanting to go to the dog park was too convenient to pass up. Being with me would give her an alibi for dosing Archie Wellington. She messed up, sort of, by miscalculating how long she'd have to sit in her car. That lapse gave her compatriots enough time to kill Archie Wellington. Of course, she didn't know that. The appearance of his severed hand came as a shock to her," I said.

Gracie wandered over and put a paw on my leg. She whined. I put my arms around her strong neck and gave her a hug. We both were thanking our lucky stars we'd found each other. If I hadn't adopted her, Gracie could have wound up in a research lab, too. That sent a shudder through me. I vowed to make more of our time together. Life's short. I needed to enjoy every minute.

Hopping to my feet, I said, "Gracie? Let's go for a walk. What do you say?"

The enthusiastic wag of her tail told me she was thrilled—and away we went.

JOANNA'S AUTHOR NOTE & FREE GIFT!

If you love traditional mysteries, pets, crafts, and friendship, you're going to love the Kiki Lowenstein Mystery Series. Kiki is a young mother struggling to make ends meet after her husband's murder. Along the way, she discovers skills she never knew she had—and she wins the heart of a hunky detective!

Claim your copy of *Love, Die, Neighbor: The Prequel to the Kiki Lowenstein Mystery Series* by going here https://BookHip.com/NVNCPV or scanning the QR code below—

ABOUT JOANNA CAMPBELL SLAN—

"Our best friend, our next-door neighbor and ourselves with just a touch of the outrageous." That's how RT Book Review describes Joanna's protagonist, Kiki Lowenstein. The truth is that's a pretty good description of Joanna as well.

Joanna is a *New York Times, USA Today,* and Amazon Best-selling author as well as a woman prone to frequent bursts of crafting frenzy, leaving her with glue gun burns and paint on her clothes. And the mess? Let's not even go there.

Otherwise, she's a productive author with more than 80 written projects to her credit. Her non-fiction work includes "how to" books, a college textbook for public speakers, and books of personal essays (five are in the Chicken Soup for the Soul books).

Learn more and sign up for her free blog by going to linktr.ee/jcslan

∽

And please add your review or rating wherever you get your books. Your comments help other readers find the right books for them.

www.ingramcontent.com/pod-product-compliance
Lightning Source LLC
LaVergne TN
LVHW012018060526
838201LV00061B/4366